Murder was in the kid's eyes.

He came flying at Peter the instant Peter was off the motorcycle, and hit him in the stomach with his shoulders like a football tackle, sending Peter crashing to the hard, blacktop surface of the parking lot.

"Hey! What're you —!" Peter started to yell, but he couldn't finish what he wanted to say. The kid — about sixteen or seventeen, dark-haired, tall and slim — was on top of him in a flash, pounding him on his face and head, mashing him with his fists.

He'll kill me! Peter thought, becoming dazed from the blows. The darned guy's gone crazy!

Covering his face with one hand, Peter made a fist of the other and drove it hard at his attacker, striking him a glancing blow on the shoulder. His next blow struck the guy on the side of his head, slowing him

1

down just long enough for Peter to roll over onto his stomach, and then crawl up onto his knees so that he was able to swing his elbows up and down like pistons in hopes of striking the kid above him on the face, or somewhere vulnerable to make the kid stop.

"Dex! Hold it! Hold it!" cried one of the two other guys standing close by, watching the fight. The ones who were really responsible for starting it.

The pounding against Peter's body ceased, leaving it throbbing with aches and pains, and he stopped flailing his elbows. He laid his hands protectively against the sides of his face and remained crouched like a fetus, his forehead resting against the hot pavement. He had to be sure the crazy fool wasn't going to start pounding him again.

The moment he felt the weight leave his back, he rolled over and sprang to his feet. He brushed his dark, disheveled hair away from his oval, suntanned face, feeling a burn on his cheek that he figured he must have sustained while lying against the pavement. For just a brief instant he glanced down at the dirt on the front of his green, zippered sport shirt and blue jeans and at his dirt-smudged white sneakers. These, and his underwear, were the only clothes he owned. Get a large tear in them and he'd be in tougher shape than he already was.

He looked up and his anxious eyes settled on the blond kid, the one wearing orange sunglasses and blue jeans. The one who had stopped the fight. The other member of the trio was a redhead. He was wearing silver reflective sunglasses and knee-length shorts, and chewing bubble gum, which he'd often blow up and pop.

The blond kid looked at Peter intensely while he motioned to Dex. Dex frowned, then approached the blond kid and bent an ear toward his mouth.

Peter watched them both intently, curiously. What did the blond have in mind now? Something worse than a beating? What could be worse?

His glance narrowed furtively on the blond, who, because of a crooked twist of his mouth and a crescent-shaped scar on his right cheek, looked meaner than the other two combined. Peter wondered how he'd gotten the scar. A knife fight?

And what about the bubble-gum popper? Was he as friendly as he looked? Or was that calm, handsome face just a mask hiding evil thoughts? Were the eyes behind the sunglasses on a constant search for mischief?

Peter could only guess, and hope that he would never do anything that would provoke all three of them into jumping on him at the same time. The thought reminded him of his own smaller stature and of his vulnerability to guys like these three. But then he remembered his battles with bigger guys back at The Good Spirit Home — the children's home in Cross Point, Florida, where he had lived most of his young life. Most of them had backed off after they discovered that they were not dealing with a spineless, chicken-livered kid, and he told himself that he wasn't going to cower from these guys either. But then he remembered where he was, and why he was here, and excused himself for not having fought back as hard against Dex as he might have.

"Hey, right! Right!" Dex exclaimed, interrupting Peter's thoughts, nodding and smiling agreeably to whatever his blond friend had said to him.

The two separated, and Dex turned and swaggered toward Peter, the smile replacing the cold, bitter look that had darkened his features earlier. He put out his hand.

"Hey, I'm sorry. All right? Guess I lost my head," he said apologetically. "Jess explained what happened. Forgive me, will you? It was all a big joke."

A big joke? Sure, it was. I'm probably going to have a black eye, and you call it a joke, Peter thought.

He glanced down at the extended hand. Finally, figuring that the guy really meant it, he took the hand and shook it.

"My friend Jess is sometimes sharper than I am," Dex went on amiably. "He just came up with a terrific idea."

Terrific idea? What? A new style of fighting?

"First, let me introduce these characters," Dex said. "This is Jess Kutter, and under this mop of red hair is Bill Rocco. I'm Dexter Pasini."

"Hi," said Peter, his voice a soft, deep drawl. He shook hands with Rocco and Kutter, neither of whom gripped his hand as firmly as he gripped theirs. "Like holding a cold fish," Mr. Fairchild, his friend back at The Good Spirit Home, used to call it when anyone shook hands like that.

5

Peter almost smiled at the thought, and just for an instant he tightened his grip on Jess Kutter's hand and saw the look of surprise come over Kutter's face, making the scar on his cheek turn white. Peter relaxed his grip and let go of the hand, wondering why he had done what he did. Well, he didn't care. Maybe the grip would tell Kutter that Peter wasn't a pushover or as weak as he might think.

Peter ran his hand through his hair, which he knew needed cutting, and felt the snarls in it as he pushed it back, trying at the same time to straighten them out to make his hair look more presentable.

"You live here in Cypress Corners?" Bill wanted to know, and popped his gum again.

"No. I'm from New York," he answered.

It was a lie. He'd never been out of Florida in his life. But he had a reason to lie, and these guys didn't have to know what it was.

Dex laughed. "How about that? New York. You're a long way from home, pal."

"Yeah."

He felt something on the corner of his mouth, took a handkerchief out of his pocket, and dabbed at it. It was blood.

"Sorry about that," Dex said.

Peter shrugged. "That's okay," he said.

He turned the bloodied spot of the handkerchief over and wiped his face with the clean part of it, rubbing harder over the high cheekbones than the strong, rounded chin that had been a haven for pimples as long as he could remember. The pimples embarrassed him. Fortunately, they never appeared anywhere else.

"How did you start my bike? That's what I'd like to know," Dex asked, curious.

Peter grinned. "With a wire."

"I know. But *how*?"

Peter shoved the handkerchief back into his pocket. "Sorry. That's my secret."

Dex's eyes blazed as he looked at Peter.

"You want me to shake it out of him, Dex?" Rocco asked, his head turning from Peter to Dex and back to Peter.

Peter braced himself. He was in no mood for another fight, but he wasn't going to stand there and take it from Rocco without fighting back either.

Dex gave Rocco a shove with his elbow. "Let me handle this, okay?" he snapped. He looked at Peter, rocked back and forth on his heels a couple of times, and said, "Pretty sharp, aren't you?" His smile, which had faded slightly, came back, even broader than before. "You own a bike?"

"No. But I've ridden them. Fixed them, too."

He wasn't lying now. He had learned a lot about bikes from Jim Fairchild, one of the maintenance men at The Good Spirit Home. Thinking back to those days seemed like it was a hundred years ago.

Dex eyed him thoughtfully for a while before he went on. "Ever raced in a moto?"

"Sure."

As a matter of fact, the most fun he'd had was in motos, or motocross meets — races conducted on a closed course that included hills, jumps (something like miniature ski jumps), rough terrain that required gear changing, and both right- and left-hand turns. He had Jim Fairchild to thank for that, too, for getting him started in them.

Dex brought out a ring of keys from his pocket, pushed a forefinger through the loop of the ring, and began to twirl it in a slow, small circle.

"How'd you like to race in one later on this morning?"

Peter stared at him. "How would I like to *what?*"

"You heard me."

"But I don't have a bike," he said, puzzled at Dex's offer.

"That's easy." Dex eyed him arrogantly. "The guy who usually rides our Una Mae is down with the flu. You can ride it. That is, if you think you can. It's a one twenty-five LC. Just like my Corella."

The Una Mae, Peter knew, was an American-made bike, considered a little bit faster than the Japanese Suzuki.

Dex pointed at his bike, which, Peter had noticed the first time he'd set eyes on it, was a real beauty. And not more than a year old. It, too, was an American-manufactured bike.

"Liquid-cooled," Peter said.

"Right. Ever ride one?"

"No. We just had two bikes, both of them air-cooled."

"The LCs are better," Dex said authoritatively. "You just have to be sure that the mixture — in the Una Mae, anyway — is fifty percent distilled water and fifty percent antifreeze. Otherwise, without the antifreeze, the water could boil and blow the tank."

"Right."

The idea of racing a bike again made Peter's heart throb. The thought that someone — a detective, or the cops — could be searching for him in Cypress Corners always lingered in the back of his mind. But that they would be looking for him right here — now — was pretty remote.

"Well? Will you or won't you?" Dex prompted him.

"I will."

Dex smiled. The other two glanced at Dex and smiled, too.

"Come on, get on behind me," Dex invited, going to his bike and climbing on it. "Hey, you guys, see you later. Okay?"

"Okay," they replied in unison.

Rocco and Kutter turned on their heels and walked away. For a moment Peter watched them, wondering if he was doing the right thing. After all, look at what those guys had done to him. Jess Kutter, specifically. Pretending that the bike belonged to him. Saying that he had lost his key. How much could you trust guys like him? Were all three like that? Birds of a feather . . .

10

Peter got on the yellow-fendered, black-tanked bike behind Dex, who put on his shiny black helmet, clicked the fasteners, then kick-started the machine.

The Corella was indeed an eye-stopper, every inch of it polished to a sheen. This baby is really given the TLC treatment — tender loving care — and it deserves every bit of it, Peter told himself.

Now Peter heard the engine roar to life, glanced back to see the smoke bursting from the twin exhausts, and then felt the bike take off gracefully, the sun reflecting off the silver spokes and cuplike hubs onto the blacktop.

He let his cares, his fears, his past drift away from him as he clung to the grips at his sides and felt the wind tangle his hair and brush past his face. There was nothing that should make him afraid of these guys, he thought. There was nothing he couldn't handle. He'd ride the Una Mae in the moto, and if the bike was as good as Dex said it was, he'd show them a thing or two.

And then he'd leave and head south, as he had planned to do. Fort Myers was his target. That was far enough from Cross Point to avoid being seen, caught, and returned to the Bentleys', the foster

11

family with whom he'd lived for the last several months.

If it wasn't, he could move on. Florida was a big state. He had studied every bit of it on a map days before he had planned his escape.

The afternoon was hot, much hotter than it had been that morning.

And the track was super. Nothing like the one near Cross Point, the Cedar Hills Speedway.

This one had more twists and turns than a pretzel factory.

Peter, riding the white-fendered, black-tanked Una Mae 125 LC, careened around a high berm with the wind humming past his helmet-covered ears. Twenty-three other bikers were scattered in the mad, roaring race around the 1.3-mile track, with him — No. 150 — somewhere among the first ten.

Now came the long stretch, and Peter lowered his shoulders and head, twisting the throttle quickly and firmly, feeling the bike's power as the rear knobbies bit into the hard dirt track and propelled the machine forward.

He sailed by No. 17, a blue-fendered 125 that had been in front of him ever since the moto had started some three laps ago. Then he crept up to a blue-tanked YZ 125 Yamaha with red-and-white striped fenders, and the number 99 emblazoned on the plate behind the seat as well as on the back of the white-helmeted rider.

Peter remembered having seen 99 scrambling for the lead from the very start of the race. Even in the densest traffic the rider, wearing a deep red, satiny suit and shiny leather boots, would stand out like a blazing torch. Maybe he had posed for a motorcycle advertisement before coming to race in the moto, Peter mused.

Peter got to within five feet of the bike, staying directly on its tail, before he made his move toward the left side of it. He gave the handle a gentle twist, got his bike out of the line made for him by the Yamaha, and started to press on by.

He saw the rider glance briefly in his direction, and for a second or two he saw that 99's eyes were wide and determined. Peter recognized from experience the spirit and dogged determination that were kindled in them.

No. 99 had probably never won a moto. Maybe he had never even placed up there among the top four or five, either spot not to be looked down upon in a motocross with twenty-four riders competing. No. 99's heart was probably set on making it this time. He wanted today to be the day that his losing streak would be broken.

But as Peter crept past 99's Yamaha, he knew that today would not be the day for 99 to win. Not unless something drastic happened to Peter, or to Dex, or to any one of those riders leading the pack.

"Good-bye, ninety-nine," he whispered as he shot by.

Another berm came up sharply, rising up along the outside of the track in a high, crest-shaped curve, although it wasn't as high as the initial one. Peter rode it side by side with two other riders.

Then — being on the inside — he careened off the berm and headed down a short stretch toward a jump-hill, the third one on the twisting, challenging track.

In spite of the many jumps he had made — some successful, some not — there was always a bit of worry that began in the pit of his stomach and stayed there till it was over, for flying off the edge of a jump-hill was no simple feat, even for an expert. The hill from which a bike took off like a skier from a ski jump was formed purposely to give variety to the track, to make the race a challenge to the rider, and provoke excitement for the spectator. Peter knew that catastrophes were always possible. He had seen them happen, although — thank goodness — he had never been involved in one himself. Sometimes they resulted in minor injuries, sometimes major ones, for the front and rear wheels had to make re-contact with the ground just right, otherwise the rider would lose his balance and control of his bike. The inevitable spill could result in critical injury to himself and damage his bike, or — as was so often the case — both rider and bike could escape the unlucky consequences and continue the race with nothing lost except precious time.

Now, as the jump-hill came up, Peter braced himself, rising off the seat as he felt the machine leave the earth and start flying through the air. His feet had left the foot rests, leaving only his hands — gripping the handlebars with steel-like fingers — in contact with the bike.

It was only a second or two that he and the Una Mae were airborne, but it seemed much longer than that to him. During that brief interval his heart seemed to have stopped, and he wondered, as he saw the ground coming up to meet him and the bike, whether the front and rear wheels would make perfect contact. If they didn't — if the front wheel came down and struck the ground at an oblique angle — it could result in a catastrophe.

Peter waited.

2

The rear wheel made contact first, and then the front, and Peter came back down upon the seat with a bump that jarred him.

He wasn't surprised. He had expected it, and he turned the handlebar slightly to the left to meet the next but lesser challenge, a curve that was wide and circled back to the right, where he was to encounter still another berm.

This one was the longest of the several on the track, but it wasn't the highest. Guys thrilled at accelerating their bikes along the length of it as if it were a straightaway.

Peter came off it like a shot as he breezed by a bike that seemed to have suddenly encountered engine trouble. Black smoke was spurting from it.

He didn't look back to see what the rider was

going to do. He just hoped that no one would run into the bike, causing injuries to its rider, and possibly to other riders.

He came upon the next high, sharp berm and had to decelerate to be able to negotiate the next couple of left- and right-hand turns without losing control of the bike.

Then came the long, final stretch, the longest on the track. Near the end of it was the finish line, and a few yards beyond it the curve that led back to the start of the racetrack.

There were still some sixteen minutes to go in the twenty-minute race; a man standing on a platform just outside of the finish line was holding up a square blackboard with the time scratched on it in white chalk. But there were other pit-board men spaced at various places around the track whose brief initialed messages kept Peter up with the time.

It was early, anyway. There was no use being concerned yet about how much more time was left in the race. What was important was to keep moving, and moving fast. There was no dillydallying, no procrastination. Every lap had to be run as if it were the last.

As he swung around the curve and back onto the wide straightaway, just ahead of the hill that the riders had to conquer when they started the race, Peter could see all the lead riders in front of him. He quickly counted seven, and recognized Dexter Pasini's yellow-fendered, black-tanked Corella 125 LC blazing away in the lead. The shiny silver spokes of the bike's wheels were dust-covered now, but the number on the back of the machine and on Dexter's back was visible, and Peter knew he would never forget it.

It was 44.

No, I can never forget it, he thought. No matter the fight, the punches, the awful names. He's letting me ride his bike, the Una Mae, a classy, little machine that fits me to a T. I won't win. I don't intend to. I don't *expect* to. But I'll have fun trying, and meanwhile, I'll not think about anything else. Nothing . . . nothing . . .

But the memory was there in the back of his mind, lurking like some worried animal wanting to get out of its hiding place but afraid to.

He had left (left? run away was more like it) the

Bentleys, his foster family in Cross Point, two days ago, gotten a ride to Tampa and then to Cypress Corners with a young couple who lived there.

They had left him off next to a mall — THE CYPRESS CORNERS MALL, the huge, neon-lighted sign at the entranceway had read — and only minutes later, as he headed toward a restaurant for a biscuit, jelly, and milk breakfast, he saw the bike, a 125 LC Corella scripted on its side.

Like a magnet it had drawn him to it, and he stood admiring it, loving it, till he heard the voice behind him say, "Hey, Bill, can you believe it? I lost my key. How am I going to start my bike without a lousy key?"

He had turned abruptly, looked behind him, and seen the two guys, the same two Dex had later introduced to him as Jess Kutter and Bill Rocco.

And, like a dummy, he had said, "I think I can start it for you."

They looked at him, genuinely surprised. The blond one, Jess, said, "You're kidding."

He smiled. They had not expected to meet one like him at all — had probably just chanced it that he might know about bikes — and clearly showed it. "All I need's a wire," he said.

He looked around and saw the back of a Goodyear garage a hundred feet away. About half a dozen garbage cans were stacked behind it, most of which were filled so much that their lids were tipped up on one side.

He went to them, searched till he found a short piece of copper wire, and returned with it to the bike. He got on the machine, reached down, and made some contacts with the wire, and the engine fired.

The guys stared at him in disbelief.

It was no big deal to him. He had done it before. Not illegally. Only when Jim Fairchild had left the keys in his office and didn't want Peter, or himself, chasing back after them. It was Jim who had shown him how to do it. That was back before he had ever heard of the Bentleys. Back when he was at the home, The Good Spirit Home in Cross Point.

He had been sitting on the bike for some thirty or forty seconds when Dex came running up from the mall, and from the angry look on his face Peter could tell immediately that he had been framed. Jess had lied to him, had deliberately lied to get him into trouble. This bike didn't belong to Jess. It belonged to the kid running toward him, face twisted with fury, eyes blazing, fists clenched. Then came the first blow, only seconds after Peter had climbed off the bike.

Now here he was, riding the Una Mae in a two-heat race on the Bumble Bee Speedway, one of the best and fastest tracks in Florida. Riding it as if the fight had never happened.

A jump-hill was coming up, and he braced himself for it. It was the highest one, and the most challenging, on the track.

3

Ahead and to the right of him was a white-fendered, black-tanked BLB 125, with a rider wearing a blue helmet and the number 11.

Peter remembered having seen the rider just before the race had started. He had looked at Peter and the three guys who were with him as they passed each other near the bike examination area. He had also spoken to the guys and had gotten a blunt greeting in return, enough to indicate to Peter that all didn't seem to be hunky-dory between him and them.

Peter had a glimpse of the rider sailing off the jump-hill in a graceful, well-balanced leap. Then he quickly placed his full attention on his own driving, and seconds later found himself soaring through space, his seat and feet free of the machine.

His eyes were on the track below him as he clung hard to the hand grips of the bike, staring with anxiety and anticipation. His breath was caught like a ball in his throat.

Then the wheels hit — the rear one first — and his feet found the pegs, and his bottom the seat, as the machine bounced and thudded down the brief incline to the level part of the track.

But suddenly the handlebars twisted to the left on him, as if the front wheel had bumped into something solid, and for an instant panic assailed him. The thought flashed through his mind that this was it, that he was going to lose control of the machine and spill.

For a second o. two he decelerated, slowing the bike down and getting the front wheel back in line without losing his balance. He had to take both feet off the pegs to do that, and lost precious time in the process.

In control again, he gave the throttle a twist and shot the bike forward, hearing the yelp that boomed from the powerful twin-cylindered engine. He took the washboard bumps in stride — so called because the track here for a hundred feet or so was grooved

like a washboard, an added variety for the riders —
and felt the forks bouncing in and out of their tubes
like a riveting machine. Peter prayed that they could
stand the gaff for the remaining twelve minutes or
so of the heat.

He had just gotten the bike well under control
again when he noticed company riding along his
right side. He took a quick glance in that direction
and saw the bright-red color of the rider's uniform.
It was the guy wearing No. 99.

He had taken advantage of Peter's brief slowdown
and had caught up to him. Now he was accelerating
his machine, trying hard to shoot by.

Peter smiled to himself and gunned the Una Mae,
giving it all the power it could take. He felt the bike
respond, could almost feel its knobbies biting into
the dirt like hungry beavers.

The Una Mae edged ahead of the Yamaha, although not as fast as he liked it to. It didn't have all
the power of a great motocrosser. It wasn't there
when you wanted it to be.

Still, he moved ahead, and by the time he reached
the first high berm, he found that he wasn't too far
behind No. 11.

On his left side now was a black-tanked Yamaha with red-and-white striped fenders. The number on it was 123, and he recognized Jess Kutter. Jess was crouched low over his bike, his rear end as far back on his seat as he possibly could get it.

Peter understood his reasoning for doing that. Putting more weight over the rear wheel meant better traction, and keeping his body low down would lessen wind resistance. Jess knew the score.

But why wasn't he farther in the lead? Maybe his bike didn't have all that get-up-and-go power to get it there, Peter thought. Or perhaps those berms and jump-hills slowed him down. The possible reasons were numerous.

Peter roared up onto the berm, heading toward the middle part of it with throttle wide open. He saw Jess Kutter coming up at his left side, maintaining a lead of only about two feet or so.

They were heading down off the berm when Peter noticed Jess cutting closer to him. From a space that was about five feet between them, Jess had narrowed it to four, then three, and was getting it even closer.

"Hey, watch it!" Peter yelled, terror seizing him for a moment.

But he held his ground. If anyone was going to yield, it was going to be Kutter, Peter told himself determinedly.

He saw Jess's head turn his way for an instant. Although he couldn't see Jess's face or eyes because of the dark gray shield, he knew that Jess could see him.

What is he up to? Is he trying to scare me? Peter thought. Is he doing that to get ahead of me?

They were nearly off the berm by now, and Peter saw Jess edging away from him, widening the gap between them.

Relief swept over him, and he wondered if Jess had deliberately ridden close to him to get him rattled. Was that one of his tricks?

Maybe he doesn't know it's me riding the Una Mae, Peter thought. Or maybe he doesn't care. Maybe he feels that just because Dex befriended me, he doesn't have to be a friend of mine, too.

Whatever Jess's intention happened to be, his ploy worked. He was ahead of Peter by about twenty feet as they streaked down the stretch toward the next berm.

Peter felt that he had been duped and was angry at himself for letting Kutter take advantage of him. Kutter was probably laughing to himself and would brag about it later to Dex.

There were only four minutes left to go in the heat when he saw two bikes collide just after they had leaped off the first jump-hill of the track. It was the track's most dangerous jump, and it was no surprise to Peter that it happened.

As a matter of fact, he was surprised that there were not more of them. It only proved that the riders were really good, he thought.

The Una Mae took the jump-hill gracefully, but Peter almost panicked as the bike landed only inches away from one of the fallen riders.

"Watch it!" he screamed as he came plunging down from the peak of the hill, the front wheel of the bike held high and the rear wheel coming down almost in the exact spot where the rider was trying to scramble out of Peter's way.

The rider — No. 14 — managed to roll out of Peter's path in time and toward his bike, which had tumbled over toward the side of the track, where bales of hay had been piled. The other fallen rider, having been on the left side of the bike he had collided into, had escaped toward the hay bales only seconds before and was now sitting with his knees hunched up, waiting for the other bikes to ride by.

A black tank and the number 123 flashed through Peter's senses as the Una Mae came to land finally on its two wheels and head on down the short stretch toward the high berm in the distance.

It was Jess Kutter's number. What had he done? Peter wondered. Had he tried to scare another rider by riding up close to him, and gotten *too* close? Maybe that accident would teach him a lesson.

But, then again, maybe it wouldn't.

Minutes later a flagman stood at the finish line and brought down the black-and-white checkered flag with a swish each time a bike sailed by him.

Peter breezed by him, too, coming in eleventh.

He was disappointed. He had hoped to come in among the first ten, at least.

4

The winner of the heat, riding his faithful Corella one twenty-five — number forty-four! Dexter Pasini!" a woman's voice announced over the public address system.

A roar burst from the crowd, then quieted down as the voice continued: "In second place, riding an Italian Jet — number one-oh-two! Jim Withers!"

Again the roar. Then the third-place winner was announced. "Riding his BLB one twenty-five and coming in third place — number eleven! Giff Mac-Kenzie!"

The roar seemed to be louder this time than it was the first two times, and Peter stood on his toes to try to see what this third-place winner, who seemed to be so popular with the fans, looked like.

He saw a tall, broad-shouldered guy about sixteen, with a thatch of blond hair topping a lean, smiling, suntanned face, waving back to the crowd. It was the kid who had spoken to Dex and his two cronies before the race and gotten a short, grunted reply in return.

"How'd she ride?" a voice broke into his thoughts.

He turned, met Dex's eyes, and smiled. "Great. But a better rider might've brought her in a lot quicker than I did."

Dex shrugged. He had his helmet off and the wind was teasing his curly black hair.

"Come on," he said. "Let's get something to drink."

Peter walked with him to the soft-drink and sandwich stand, carrying under his arm the helmet Dex had also let him borrow.

As a matter of fact, nearly everything he wore Dex was letting him borrow: the helmet, the gloves, the shoes, and the uniform. Never mind that they were battle-scarred; they were still usable.

Following close behind them were Jess Kutter and Bill Rocco. Jess had gotten back on his bike after the collision and finished the heat, coming in fourteenth. Peter didn't know what had happened to the other rider. He probably hadn't finished.

31

Jess hadn't said anything to Peter about that close-driving incident on the high berm, nor to Dex. Peter said nothing, too. Better that it be forgotten, he thought, than bring it up and cause an argument.

They walked up to the counter, and Dex turned to Jess, a broad smile coming over his dimple-cheeked, suntanned face.

"Okay, pal. Your turn to spring," he said.

Jess stared at him, seemed on the verge of arguing the point, then lowered his gaze and dug into his back pocket for his wallet. Somehow, Peter got the feeling that Jess never argued with Dex. That whatever Dex said, went.

"What time does the second heat start?" Peter asked.

"Two o'clock." Dex drained his Coke, set the empty can on the counter, and waved to Peter and his two friends. "Come on. Let's gas up the bikes."

Dex had brought along a five-gallon container of gasoline on the pickup that had carted their three bikes to the track, and he refilled the tanks. He had also fetched a box of new sparkplugs, and asked Peter to make the replacements.

Why me? Peter wanted to ask him, wondering

why they each couldn't do the simple job themselves.

But he said nothing and removed the plugs with a
wrench, then replaced them with the new ones.

Once he saw Dex in a close huddle with Jess and
Bill, and saw them looking intently at him, speaking
in soft tones. He felt certain they were talking about
him, but he couldn't hear what they were saying.

When he was finished tightening the last plug,
Dex slapped him playfully on the shoulder. "Thanks,
old buddy. You're fitting in just great. You know
that?"

Peter shrugged. Dex didn't know that Peter
couldn't fit in just great with anything. Not for long,
anyway. Soon after the moto was over, Peter had to
move on. He wanted to be in Fort Myers before
dark.

Peter put the tool back into the kit, took out a
soiled cloth, wiped his hands with it, then put it back
and locked the kit.

"Like another drink?" Dex asked.

"No, thanks. I've had enough," Peter said.

He picked up his helmet and stuck it under his
right armpit. For a long moment he stared off

toward the stadium seats of the track and felt that he was in a trance.

He just couldn't believe that he was here, racing in a motocross. He was supposed to be on the run, not accepting favors like riding somebody else's bike in a race. This was crazy.

But he was into it up to his ears now. Too deep to back out till it was over.

He heard the same woman's voice coming over the public address system again, and he shifted his thoughts to listen to what she was saying.

"Riders, please get in your places at the starting gate," she said. "The second heat will start in five minutes."

As before, the hill was the first item on the bill to conquer, and nineteen bikes crossed the starting gate and headed for it as if their lives depended on it. And somehow they did, for, as Peter knew, conquering the hill meant that you had a good chance of finishing the race. *Not* conquering it meant that you had no chance at all.

The roar of the engines was deafening as the bikes

raced side by side up the hill. Peter had the throttle wide open and could feel the knobbies tearing up the dirt as the machine scrambled up the incline.

Near the peak of it the Una Mae seemed to lose power. Then it came almost to a dead stop, and Peter yelled at it, "Don't stop now! For crying out loud, don't stop now!"

He worked the throttle feverishly, feeding the much-needed gas back into the carb and then to the plug upon which the life of the machine depended so much. He felt the power surge through the bike as the rear knobbies caught traction and spun, pushing the vehicle up to the peak and then over it.

A thrill swept through Peter as the machine picked up speed, then roared down the hill, Peter bending as low as he could to cut the wind resistance down to a minimum.

The Una Mae reached the bottom of the hill, its front end surging up slightly to meet the beginning of the flat, long straightaway. Peter saw a dozen bikes ahead of him and quickly tried to recognize them. The first one that captured his attention was

99, the rider next to him — the guy in the crimson suit riding the blue-tanked Yamaha. Peter glanced ahead and saw No. 123 — Jess Kutter — in about sixth place. No. 44 — Dex — was in about fourth.

Peter took the high berm that came up, roared down it at accelerated speed, and headed down the straightaway.

There were eleven minutes left to go, according to one of the pit boards a guy was holding up for his rider to see, when Peter saw a familiar white-fendered BLB blazing down the stretch alongside a yellow-fendered, black-tanked Corella. The two of them were scrambling for the lead: Giff MacKenzie on the BLB, Dex Pasini on the Corella.

Then, as they headed for the berm, Peter saw the Corella make a short, jerking turn toward the BLB, and the BLB swinging away from it and almost losing control. The bikes were zooming up onto the berm now, with MacKenzie on the upper side of it and Dex below him.

The move — dirty and tricky, in Peter's opinion — had helped Dex gain at least a couple of yards on

MacKenzie, and Peter wondered if he'd get away with it.

Perhaps he would, Peter thought. Dex had made the slick move quickly and furtively, and unless a track marshal had had his eyes on him, he would not have noticed it. It was only by coincidence that Peter had happened to glance that way at the exact moment that the incident had occurred, otherwise he would not have seen it either.

There were eight minutes left to go when Peter realized that he had an excellent chance of coming in among the top four. Dex, No. 44, was leading; No. 16 was second; MacKenzie, No. 11, was third; and No. 123 was fourth. In fifth place, trailing only by a yard, was Peter.

A thought went through his mind now that had repeated itself many times in the past when he was riding in just such a position: At this point take them one at a time. Concentrate on passing the rider immediately ahead of you, then work on the next. Never mind where the lead rider is. Work on him when you reach him.

The idea was a good one, even though it didn't

always work out. It was a strategy that Mr. Fairchild had taught him. The strategy usually worked for him, Mr. Fairchild had said. If things went right, it should work for Peter as well.

It did — but not often.

It didn't now. Peter had almost forgotten about No. 99, whose bike he had passed sometime back. Suddenly there it was again, coming up on his left side, the crimson suit like a blazing flame. And then it zipped by him as if he were standing still. He could hardly believe it.

The number, 99, flashed back at him in the sunlight like a wink of mockery.

It was near the first jump-hill of the track where he finally caught up with 99 again. The rider seemed to have decelerated slightly before reaching it, as if he feared the high, long flight through space and the hard, solid re-contact with mother earth.

No. 99 was already soaring through space when Peter reached the edge of the jump-hill, but his full attention was on his own flight now. Peter's speed and momentum were carrying him far out upon the track, perhaps farther out than he had ever traveled at any time before this.

Peter was about halfway in his flight when he realized that he was going to have problems. The bike had turned a little coming off the peak of the jump-hill. Not much, but enough to inject a bit of fear into him, and the strong feeling that this jump was going to be a disaster.

He turned his wheel to keep it in line with the direction in which he was going, and waited for the rear wheel to hit. Suddenly Peter felt it make contact, even though the only parts of his body that were touching the bike were his hands on the handlebars.

Then the front wheel hit, the impact forcing the front forks to plunge down to their full 11.8-inch limit inside the hefty 28-mm tubes. His rear end came down upon the saddle seat so hard that he felt the coiled springs pressing down to their limit, heard their groaning protest from his weight. Then Peter sensed the machine being out of balance under him, and he knew — even before it happened — that he was going to spill. He just couldn't help it now.

Peter twisted the throttle back almost to stopping position as he felt the bike falling away from under him. He waited till it was nearly on its side before he let go of the handlebars, hit the dirt, and rolled over onto the track away from it, and from any bikes that were making the long leap over the jump-hill.

Landing up against a stack of hay, Peter quickly leaped to his feet. He felt bruises on both of his arms, but that was all. Nothing else hurt him. Nothing, he was sure, was broken.

Peter looked for his bike, and saw it lying on its side some twenty feet down the track away from him. It was about seven or eight feet inside of the track from the same side that he was on, and one biker had already run into it. The guy was still hanging on to his machine, pulling it upright, and getting back on it. He was already on his way by the time Peter saw his own way clear to go after the Una Mae.

Peter didn't know how many bikes had gone by him by the time he reached the Una Mae, climbed on it, and got it going again. He was sure there weren't more than five or six.

So where would that leave him if he finished the race and didn't lose any more ground? In tenth place, maybe? Eleventh?

It didn't matter. He would finish it, no matter where he ended up. Luckily the Una Mae wasn't damaged.

The minutes drifted by, and finally the twenty minutes were up. Peter crossed the finish line only a foot behind an orchid-colored Honda.

Moments later the announcement came over the public address system: "Ladies and gentlemen, winner of the second heat is, you guessed it, number forty-four! Dexter Pasini! Can't anybody ever beat him?"

Cheers exploded from the hundreds of fans. And, among them, a smattering of boos.

Peter heard the names of the second- and third-place winners announced, neither of which was familiar to him.

But in fourth place was No. 11, Giff MacKenzie. A thunderous applause followed.

From the corner of his eye he saw a head turn in his direction. He looked and saw Dex peering avidly at him.

"Come on," Dex said, motioning to him. "Let's get out of here. You and I have things to talk about."

Peter frowned at him. What things? he wanted to ask.

They lifted the three bikes onto the pickup, chained them to their stands, then climbed into the vehicle and took off. Dex drove. Peter sat on the passenger-door side and Jess in the middle.

"Two in a row," Peter exclaimed as they rode out of the speedway onto the main highway. "Wowee, man. That's good driving."

Kutter laughed. "Heck, he does it all the time."

"No, not all the time," Dex contradicted. "I finished second in a heat last week and seventh in a heat a month ago. I'll take credit, but only when it's due me."

"Not bad credit," Peter said, smiling.

There was no more said for quite a while, and he thought about the statement that Dex had made to him earlier.

"What do you want to talk to me about, Dex?" he asked finally.

Dex shrugged. "Let's have something to eat first. Okay? I'm starving."

"Guess I'll have to pass on that," Peter said. "I'm down to my last two bucks."

Dex glanced at his reflection in the rear-view mirror. "Pete, you worry too much, you know that? How would you like to own that bike you rode today? You did a great job riding it. I think I can talk my uncle into letting you have it."

Peter stared back at him. (He couldn't believe he had heard right.) "Say that again."

Dex laughed and repeated what he'd said.

He's kidding, Peter thought. He must be. Nobody would offer to give a bike to a kid the first day he saw him — whether he rode well or not.

"I don't know. I've got to have a place to sleep," Peter said. "That means I've got to find a job."

"No problem." Peter saw Dex look at Kutter. "Right, Jess? You think Pete's going to have a problem finding a job?"

Jess chuckled. "No problem at all."

Twenty-five minutes later they pulled up into the parking lot of the Cypress Corners Mall. Dex drove toward the long row of light-emblazoned buildings, reached the end of the driveway, then cut sharply to the right.

At the extreme end of the mall was the Pasini Bike Shop. About ten new motorcycles and half a dozen sparkling-clean minicarts were displayed in a space next to it.

"We unload the bikes, eat, then talk," said Dex authoritatively. "Okay?"

He shot Peter a grin as he unlatched his door and got out. Peter tried to fathom the grin. What was behind it? he wondered. What did Dex Pasini really have in mind?

5

We've got a good thing going, but we can use another hand. Yours."

Dex smiled. He hadn't smiled since they had entered the restaurant, where they each had had a beef stroganoff dinner.

He had seemed to be thinking a lot about something, as if assembling certain thoughts in his mind and making sure they were in the right order before he started to explain them.

"For what?" Peter asked, curious.

Already he was beginning to feel nervous about what Dex was going to say. Somehow he wished he hadn't accepted Dex's offer to race. But that was behind him now. There was nothing he could do but hear Dex out.

They were outside of the shop, behind the motorcycles and the minicarts. Down to the left of them, facing the main street, was a bank. From where he stood Peter couldn't see a single person, only the dozens of parked cars, and the cars driving back and forth on the street beyond.

All at once he felt very lonely, and helpless. There wasn't a soul he knew in Cypress Corners except these two guys, Dex Pasini and Jess Kutter. He knew Bill Rocco, too, but only vaguely. More vaguely than he knew Dex and Jess.

And he knew Giff MacKenzie, but by sight only.

That was all. The few friends that he had lived in Cross Point, some seventy-five miles away. Up beyond St. Petersburg. And he might never see them again.

The thought left a hollow sensation in the pit of his stomach in spite of the big meal that he had put away only a little while ago. If something happened to him, to whom could he turn? No one.

"I let you take a bike to ride, right?"

Dex's voice jarred him from his reverie. "Right. And I appreciate it."

"I paid for your entry fee, and then for the dinner. Right?"

Peter nodded, frowning. "Right."

What was Dex leading up to? He was getting Peter more nervous by the minute.

"And you want a place to sleep tonight. Right?"

Again Peter nodded. Come to the point, Dex, he thought. What are you trying to say?

Dex stepped up closer to him and put an arm around his shoulder. "How'd you like to earn twenty-five percent of every buck we bring in, Pete?"

Peter met his eyes. Who do I have to kill? he wanted to say. "Doing what?" he asked.

Dex glanced at Kutter, then again at Peter. "We're in the car-parts operation, Pete," Dex explained, speaking almost directly into Peter's left ear. "We relieve certain cars of hubcaps, radios, CBs, tape decks, and now and then batteries. It is, like the big shots say, a lucrative business."

Peter's heart began to pound like crazy, causing the last few words of Dex's to drone in his ears. Stealing? Is that what Dex wanted him to do? Oh, God!

47

His spine turned into a stick of ice. What Dex was suggesting brought dark, vivid memories back to him. Back at The Good Spirit Home he had stolen some stuff — cigarettes (for a couple of his friends, since he didn't like to smoke) and money. That was all. The first time was easy. The second was even easier. But the third time he got caught.

His punishment was ten whacks with a paddle done by Dr. Forrest Cunningham himself, the director of the home. A giant of a man, six-foot-four, and cold as an iceberg, Dr. Cunningham seemed more concerned about discipline for the students than about injured feelings. Each whack, Peter remembered, seemed hard enough to snap every bone in his body. He could never understand why none of them did.

Peter was also confined in the home with no privileges to watch television, listen to radio, or get near a bike for a whole month. He had seen Mr. Fairchild only once in all that time. He also had to spend two hours every afternoon painting the halls of the home, and if he were caught talking with any of the kids, the length of his punishment would be extended accordingly. He had no idea of what life in prison was like, but that was a taste of it that he didn't want a part of anymore.

"Forget it, Dex," he said, raising his hand. He had heard enough of Dex's proposition. "That's not for me."

He looked at Dex, saw the dark, piercing expression that came into his eyes, then looked at Jess. The ice-cold sidelong glance that he got back in return told him that that wasn't the answer they expected from him.

"But it *is* for you, Pete," Dex declared, keeping his voice low and steady. "Starting tonight."

He was smiling now, as if he were sure that this time Peter's reply would be in the affirmative.

"Sorry," Peter said, and started to head toward the parking lot.

It was about five-thirty, he guessed. If he started to hitchhike now, he should be able to make it to Fort Myers long before dark.

"Just a minute, Pete," Dex said.

Peter paused and turned around. He saw it coming, but it was too quick for him to do anything about it.

Dex's fist got him in the stomach, doubling him

over and filling him with pain and nausea that made him want to vomit. He got dizzy, closed his eyes, and clutched at his stomach. He thought he was going to pass out. He lay down and rolled over onto his side, the pain of the blow feeling like an explosion inside of him.

"Come on, Jess," he heard Dex say as if from a long distance away. "Let's get out of here."

A few seconds later he heard their motorbikes start up, and then the roar of their engines as they sped away.

He lay with the side of his face flat against the hot pavement, his knees drawn up against his hurt stomach, and began to cry.

I wish I were dead, he thought.

He should have known that Dex had a reason for letting him borrow a bike and all that gear and encouraging him to enter the motocross. Dex must have gathered, from the ease with which Peter had fixed his bike, and from what Peter had told him about his experiences working on and riding bikes in motos, that Peter was an excellent prospect for his "operation."

And, since Peter had run away from a foster home

and had no place to go, how could Peter *not* accept Dex's offer to join his operation?

But he couldn't steal again. He *wouldn't* steal again. Never. And he certainly would not join an operation like Dex's.

He couldn't believe it. How long did Dex think he could get away with stealing hubcaps and all that other stuff? Didn't it ever occur to him what a stiff fine, and a jail term, meant if he got caught?

"Kid! Are you hurt?"

The voice cut into his thoughts, startling him for a moment.

He opened his eyes and looked up at someone bending over him. A young man with friendly blue eyes, a cheerful, suntanned face, and a thatch of wavy blond hair.

Where have I seen him before? Peter asked himself.

"Did they hurt you?" the guy asked.

He recalled where he had seen the face now, and that mop of blond hair. At the motocross. It was one of the riders.

"Can you get up?"

Without answering, Peter put a hand against the

pavement and pushed himself up. The guy helped him.

Peter stood on his feet, waiting to see if he'd get dizzy again. He still felt nauseated, but not as much as he had earlier.

"I'm Giff MacKenzie," the guy introduced himself. "I spoke to you at the track."

"I know. I recognized you."

Peter looked down at his clothes, saw the dirt on one side of them, and brushed it off.

"Why'd they hit you?" Giff asked.

"They didn't both hit me," Peter said. "Only Dex did."

"Why?"

"He wanted me to join his outfit."

"That's what I thought." Giff didn't elaborate. He probably knew what kind of an outfit Dex had. "You're new here, aren't you?"

Peter nodded. "I got here this morning, and I'm leaving now."

He glanced toward the sky. The sun was still high above the horizon, spraying bursts of yellow rays from behind a cloud. He glanced at the street, where traffic was still flowing briskly.

"Where you going?"

Peter opened his mouth to answer, met Giff's eyes, and felt a ball rise in his throat.

"What's your name?" Giff asked.

"Peter. Peter Lewinski."

"I'd like to help you, Peter," Giff said.

Peter stared at him. A Good Samaritan? He couldn't believe it. "Why?"

"This was no coincidence my coming here and finding you," Giff explained. "I was at one of the stores when I saw you walking out of the restaurant with Dex Pasini and that buddy of his, Jess Kutter."

Peter brushed back his hair with his fingers. "You watched us?"

"Yes, I did. I watched you guys come here. But the three of you went behind this building, out of my sight, and I didn't want to get out there in the parking lot where Dex and Jess could see me, so I just hung back and waited. Then I saw them come out from here without you and take off on their bikes."

"Why?" Peter asked again, looking into Giff's blue eyes with deep curiosity. "What business is it of yours what they do, or what I do?"

53

Giff shrugged. "No business, I guess. Maybe I just want to help."

"How well do you know Dex?"

"Well enough to know that I'd trust a snake quicker than I'd trust him."

Giff paused. Peter looked at him, squinting a little against the sunlight, waiting for him to go on.

"Look, can we sit and talk?" Giff asked him. "Over a Coke, maybe?"

"I haven't got time," Peter said. "I've got to —"

"How'd you get mixed up with Dex, anyway?" Giff cut in. "What did you do to get him to let you ride one of his bikes in the moto? You must've done *something.*"

"I was tricked."

"Tricked?" Giff frowned.

"Yes." And Peter went on to tell him about arriving at the Cypress Corners Mall, seeing the Corella 125 LC bike, admiring it, then Jess and Bill stopping by and conning him into making him believe that the Corella was Jess's, that he couldn't start it, and Peter ending up starting it for him with a wire he had found in a garbage can.

"Tricked? You were suckered," Giff said, shaking

his head. "Either one of those goons would pull a fast one on his own mother."

"Then, while I'm sitting on the bike —"

"Dex shows up."

"And the war starts."

Peter glanced toward the mall. Somewhere there should be a clock. What time was it getting to be, anyway?

He looked back at Giff and saw a black digital watch on his left wrist.

"What time is it?" he asked. "I can't hang around much —"

"Five-oh-five," Giff said, glancing at the time, and went on quickly, "Look, how do you know so much about motorcycles?"

Peter had started to turn away. He was getting nervous, fidgety. He wanted to leave. He *had* to leave. Now.

"My father had one," he said, lying through his teeth. "He was also a mechanic. He taught me everything I know."

"I figured it was something like that. How about working on mine?"

"What?"

"Working on my bike," Giff explained, smiling. "I've been finishing up behind the winners, but I know I could come up a winner if my BLB had all the kinks taken out of it."

"Can't. I'm sorry, I just can't," said Peter. But he found himself gazing past Giff's shoulders at the huge lot behind him in an effort to spot the BLB 125 he could remember so well.

"Why can't you?" Giff asked, pressing him. "What's your hurry? Where are you going?"

That's my business, Peter wanted to say as he turned his gaze back to Giff. (He hadn't been able to see the BLB. There were too many cars in the lot to try to see through.) But he restrained himself from saying that, knowing he'd regret it if he did. Giff seemed like a nice guy. Friendly and tolerant.

"I'm heading for Fort Myers," Peter said.

"Got relatives there?"

Peter met Giff's deep-blue, piercing eyes. "No. No relatives," he answered calmly. "I just want to go there, that's all."

Giff cleared his throat. "You in trouble, Pete?"

Peter's eyes widened for a second. Then he grinned, not too surprised. After all, he certainly must have shown enough signs to indicate that all was not well with him.

"Sort of," he admitted. "But I didn't commit any crime, if that's what you're thinking. I — I just ran away from a place. A foster home."

"From where?"

"Cross Point."

Peter felt the piercing blue eyes probing him, and he wanted to turn and go on his way. Yet something detained him, urging him to reconsider Giff's offer to fix his bike. Peter could ask Giff to let him take a shower at his place afterward. That wouldn't be too much to ask for payment, would it? Maybe his clothes wouldn't be very clean, but he would be.

"I've got an idea," Giff cut into his thoughts. "Come home with me, fix my bike, take a good hot shower, then stay overnight. After breakfast tomorrow morning, you can decide whether you want to head for Fort Myers or not. That sound good to you?"

Peter broke out laughing. Had Giff read his mind?

He was about to say okay when the roar of a motorcycle cut sharply into his senses. He turned toward the direction of the street where the sound was coming from and saw a blue-fendered, blue-tanked bike heading toward them. The rider was wearing blue jeans, white leather gloves, shiny brown leather boots, and a milk-white helmet.

No. 99!

Even though the rider wasn't wearing his familiar crimson suit and number now, Peter remembered him. The guy had given him some tough moments out there on the track.

"It's D.C.," Giff said, smiling.

The rider rode the bike up toward them, shut off the ignition, and started to take off his helmet.

When the visored white helmet came off, a mass of long, nut-brown hair tumbled down against slender shoulders.

"Hi!" the girl greeted the boys cheerfully. "Making secret plans for the next moto?"

Peter stared, flabbergasted.

Giff laughed.

"Pete," he said, "meet D.C., my sister."

6

Hi," Peter said, cracking a smile.

He was surprised, bashful, nervous. This was the first chance he had of really getting a good look at her face, and she was beautiful. Her round cheeks were slightly pink, as was the tip of her slightly up-tilted nose. Her lips were almost as red and shiny as the uniform she had worn in the race, and Peter wondered if she was wearing lipstick.

"This is Peter Lewinski," Giff said. "He just had a falling out with Dex and company."

"Oh?"

D.C. looked at Peter's black eye, then at his hair, which he knew must look like a rat's nest, then at his clothes, and finally back at his eyes again. Her own brown eyes, below long, dark lashes, were guarded now, as if she didn't quite know what to make of him.

"You had a fight with Dex?"

Peter shrugged. "Sort of. He got the best of me, as you can see."

"What happened?"

"Look," Giff interrupted, "why don't we head for home? Pete's going to fix up my BLB, take the roughness out of it. Maybe he'll have a chance to tell you all about it tonight. Okay?"

D.C. stared at Giff, then at Peter, her cheeks reddening like ripened apples. "He's coming to *our* house?" she said, as if Giff were inviting a dirty nogood bum he had found lying on a street to go home with him.

"Yes, D.C.," Giff replied, a sharp change in his otherwise calm, soft voice. "I invited him. He's going to fix my bike. That all right with you?"

The sudden exchange made Peter uncomfortable. He turned and walked off toward the sidewalk that ran along the mall, hurt that he should be the cause for the spat between Giff and D.C.

"Peter, wait!"

The call came from Giff. Peter paused, not sure now what to do. Should he still accept Giff's invitation in spite of what D.C. had said?

He turned and glanced at her and saw her looking at his legs. Her eyes rose quickly, wide and glistening, her mouth pressed in a hard, tight line. She's probably noticed that I've got one leg shorter than the other, Peter thought. Should that make me different from anybody else? Look, girl, he ached to tell her, I can't help that I'm a cripple. I didn't ask to be born like this.

Peter turned to Giff, his hands shoved angrily into his empty pockets. "No, Giff," he said, trying hard to control his voice. "I better go. Thanks, but —"

"No. Please," D.C. cut in, penitently. "I'm sorry." She looked at both of them pleadingly, her eyes blinking as if she were ready to cry. "I didn't mean anything. I really didn't." She put her helmet back on and climbed onto her bike. "I'll see you both later. 'Bye!"

Peter watched her take off, wheeling the Yamaha in a slow, sharp U-turn that got her directed back toward the street.

"Don't let her bother you," Giff said. "I just surprised her, that's all. She still might think you're a friend of Dex and his buddies." Giff flung an arm around Peter's shoulders. "Come on. Let's go."

Peter hung back. "No, Giff. I really don't think —"

"Hey!" Giff interrupted, looking at him, a smile brightening his blue eyes. "Come on, will you? You can't be going anywhere else now, anyway. It's too late."

"But D.C. doesn't want me at the house, Giff," Peter said firmly. "No matter what she said before she left, she still doesn't."

"She'll change her mind as soon as she knows more about you," Giff said, insistent. "I know her. She's a hard-willed girl, but I know my sister. She's going to be so sorry for acting like she did toward you that she'll come apologizing. You wait and see."

Peter studied Giff's warm, friendly face, pondered Giff's words. No, he thought. D.C. would never apologize to him. Giff was merely trying to salve his hurt feelings.

But if he left now, Peter thought, she would always think of him as being a bum, the type of guy who belonged with people like Dex, Jess, and Bill. Could he live with that thought nagging at the back of his mind? Peter didn't think so. Best that he accept Giff's invitation. Maybe after D.C. got to know him better, she'd realize she was wrong about him.

If she wanted to apologize to him then, okay. He wouldn't care one way or another. He'd just be relieved to know that she no longer considered him in a class with Dex and his friends.

"Okay," he said to Giff, cracking a smile. "I'll go with you."

Giff smiled back and extended a hand. "Thanks, Pete," he said, and they shook on it. Then they headed briskly for the sidewalk that stretched like a wide ribbon down the full length of the mall, Peter finding that he had to accelerate his pace to keep up with Giff's long-legged strides.

"What does D.C. stand for?" Peter asked, curious.

"Dorothy Catherine," Giff answered. "She was named after our grandmother."

About halfway down the sidewalk Giff stepped off the curb and headed toward the parking lot, Peter trailing him. Giff's motorcycle — still dirty from racing in the motocross — was parked in a slot next to one reserved for the handicapped.

Giff had left his helmet hanging over the left handlebar. He took it off and pulled it on, then fastened its straps. Giff mounted the bike and Peter climbed on behind him.

Giff inserted the key into the ignition, turned it, then jumped onto the starting pedal, kick-starting the engine. The bike popped after the second try. Then Giff raised the kick stand with a short upward jab of his right foot and gently turned the bike around. He twisted the hand grip and rode the bike down the lane to the street.

A soft, sputtering sound in the engine caught Peter's trained ear. Either the sparkplug was loaded up or the carburetor needed a minor adjustment, he figured. Other than that the bike rode like a breeze.

Giff paused at the mouth of the driveway, waited till two cars drove by, then turned onto the street, headed north.

"I noticed that you walk with a limp, Pete, as if one leg's shorter than the other," Giff observed, talking over his shoulder.

"That's right, it is," Peter replied.

He hadn't given his legs a thought until a little while ago when D.C. had seemed to notice it, and now he was surprised that Giff mentioned it. Few people ever did.

"Born that way?" Giff asked.

"Yes."

They rode down the street for several blocks, then turned right onto Casper Boulevard, crossed a bridge over the intercoastal waterway, and rode on.

D.C. was nowhere in sight.

Peter smelled an obnoxious odor that reminded him of rotten eggs, then saw a sewage plant about four hundred yards away to his left. By the time they reached the red light at the intersection and stopped, he was no longer aware of the smell.

They crossed Route 41, heading east, and about a mile farther on Giff turned left onto Laurel Street. He made two more turns onto streets flanked by one- and two-story homes, palm trees, and other tropical shrubbery, then drove up onto the driveway of number 1641, slowed down, and stopped.

Peter was impressed by the yellow, two-story home with white shutters on the windows and two white, round pillars on the front porch. White-painted steps led up to the porch, and a giant oak tree grew in the front yard, its gnarled branches stretching out over the roof of the house. D.C.'s bike was parked in front of the two-car garage.

Suddenly Peter felt apprehensive about coming here. The clothes he wore — a green sport shirt, blue jeans with dirt scuffs on them from the fight with Dex, and worn sneakers — were not the best a kid could impress the parents of a kid like Giff with. But he was here now; there was nothing he could do about it.

Giff pushed the bike up next to his sister's, pulled the kick stand out with his foot, laid the bike against it, then invited Peter into the house.

"I want you to meet my mother," he said. "My father won't be home till five-thirty. He's an investment broker."

Peter had no idea what an investment broker did. He had never heard the term before.

I wonder what my father did when he was alive, he thought. Nobody ever told me. All Peter knew was that he was about two years old when he was riding in a car with his parents. The car was struck by a train at a railroad crossing and both of his parents were killed. Miraculously, he was spared.

Unfortunately, he had no living relative and had to be left in a home for children — The Good Spirit Home in Cross Point, which wasn't far from St. Petersburg, where Peter and his family used to live. It had been no picnic, those fourteen years at The

Good Spirit Home. Dr. Forrest Cunningham ran the place with extra-strict discipline, meting out punishment to the offenders, using his wooden paddle unflinchingly on any kid caught smoking or stealing — an experience Peter had had himself, and which sometimes had almost caused him to run away from there.

Then came the day that Dr. and Mrs. Bentley visited the home, looking for a child to keep them and their only son — 190-pound, eighteen-year-old Tommy Joe — company. They saw Peter, liked him, and after two weeks of waiting for legal papers to be signed, they took Peter home with them.

Living with the Bentleys wasn't so bad at first. Both Dr. Bentley and his wife were not home very much. Besides the doctor's profession keeping him away a lot, he and Mrs. Bentley were very much occupied with social affairs. Their absence from home left Peter alone with Tommy Joe, which was really why, Peter soon discovered, the Bentleys had wanted him. They didn't want Tommy Joe to be left alone. Mrs. Bentley had told Peter that a baby-sitter had taken care of Tommy Joe all these years, but after Tommy Joe had grown up he didn't need a sitter anymore. He needed a male companion to keep him company, to play video games with, to go to school sports events with, and so on.

That was all right, until Tommy Joe had begun to tease Peter, to wrestle with him and use him for a punching bag. Tommy Joe was a junior in high school, but he wasn't able to make any of the athletic teams he tried out for.

Then one day Tommy Joe found his father's liquor, drank half a bottle, and tried to persuade Peter to drink some of it, too. Peter refused, so Tommy Joe got mad and tried to force Peter to drink it by pinning his arms back and pouring the liquor down his throat. What happened next was a page in Peter's life story that he was sure he'd never forget. In their struggle, he and Tommy Joe had ended up near the fireplace. Tommy had almost forced Peter to drink the liquor when Peter turned and saw a pair of iron tongs — the kind used to turn logs in a fireplace. He grabbed them desperately with one hand and struck Tommy Joe on the shoulder, missing his head by inches.

Tommy Joe had let out a yell and staggered back

onto the floor, where he fell and lay for a minute, his eyes searching Peter's wildly.

"I'll kill you for this! I'll kill you!" Tommy Joe had yelled.

That was when Peter knew he had to get out, to leave before Tommy Joe would have a chance to get up and make his threat real. That was two days ago.

Now, as Peter followed Giff into the blue-carpeted, tastefully furnished living room, he felt almost in a daze. Life with the Bentleys seemed of another time, another world.

A woman with frost-white, wavy hair was sitting on a yellow-and-blue patterned sofa, reading a magazine. She looked up as the two boys entered, and Peter saw her eyes — blue as Giff's — gaze immediately at his face, then at his clothes, at his hair, and finally at his black eye. Peter blushed.

"Mom, this is Peter Lewinski," Giff said. "I invited him over to fix my bike. Pete, meet my Mom."

Peter extended his hand. Mrs. MacKenzie got to her feet, so that she was at eye-level with him in her low-heeled shoes, and shook his hand. Her slim, sensitive face broke into a warm smile.

"So nice to meet you, Peter," she said.

"It's nice to meet you, too, Mrs. MacKenzie," Peter replied.

Her eyes settled on his black eye again. "Dear, are you all right?" she asked plaintively.

"Yes. I'm okay," he said.

Peter hoped she wouldn't begin to ask him a lot of embarrassing questions, like about where he lived and whether he had friends in Cypress Corners. He wasn't ready for anything like that just yet.

"D.C. told me you were coming," Mrs. MacKenzie said. Her voice was slightly on the husky side, Peter thought, as if she were getting over a cold. "I'm glad you came, Peter. You're staying for dinner, aren't you?"

"Well, I —" Peter started to say.

"Yes, and he's staying overnight, too," Giff cut in, grinning. "That'll be okay, won't it, Mom?"

Mrs. MacKenzie's eyebrows raised in surprise, and she glanced from him to Peter. "Why, I suppose it is. We have a guest room," she said evenly.

She started to look at Peter's dirty pants when suddenly there was a sound of footsteps coming down a stairway. Her eyes lifted and swept past his shoulders.

Peter turned and felt the blood rush to his face. It was D.C. She was wearing a dress now — a pink one with a white belt — giving Peter his first chance to see her legs.

"Hi, again," D.C. said, smiling. Faking it, he thought.

"Hi," he said.

Her hair was parted in the middle, with bangs in front. Peter glanced back at Mrs. MacKenzie, noticed the similarity in their faces again, and looked back at D.C. He tried to relax, to keep his breathing steady and quiet, but found it difficult.

She had reached the bottom of the stairs and now stood there, one arm around the round nub of the post, the toe of her left foot still on the bottom step.

Peter saw her look across the room to her mother, and could almost read the message that flashed in it. *Well, Mother. What do you think of him?* they were asking.

Peter's heart cooled. He couldn't mistake that look. She had acted coldly toward him at the mall. She was acting just as coldly toward him now.

"Darling, I think that you and I should have a little talk," Mrs. MacKenzie said in a warm, subdued voice to her daughter. Her smile showed lovely white teeth and enhanced a dimple in her chin that was barely noticeable before. "After the boys leave. Okay?"

D.C.'s face colored slightly. "If you think so, Mother."

Mrs. MacKenzie looked at Giff, then at Peter. The smile was still fresh on her face. "I'll call you when dinner's ready," she said and headed for the kitchen.

"Come on, Pete," said Giff, and followed his mother to the kitchen. Then he entered a side door into the garage, Peter behind him. A dirt-smeared, ivory-colored VW was parked on the left side of it. An array of tools lined a pegboard on the front wall, and in front of it was a workbench that was either fairly new or had not been used very much.

Giff pressed a button near the kitchen door. The wide double doors in front opened, and he went out and wheeled in his bike, then D.C.'s.

Peter found a sparkplug socket wrench and unscrewed the plug from the engine, figuring he'd look at that first. Judging by the rough sound that he had heard from the engine, he felt certain that the plug could stand a cleaning, or even a replacement.

He looked closely at the points, saw that they were badly corroded, and decided that a new one was definitely needed. He suggested it to Giff, who agreed with him.

He screwed the plug back in, then took off the carburetor. He saw that it needed an overhauling, and he promptly got the proper tools and started to work on it.

After he had the carburetor finished and re-installed, he recalled something else about the bike that he had noticed while he was riding pinion behind Giff over some of the rough spots in the streets.

"During races, have you noticed the front end of the bike jumping a lot?" he asked Giff.

Giff thought a moment, frowned, and nodded. "Why, yes, now that you mention it. It bounces a lot. But I hadn't thought —"

"I think your forks need air. Maybe oil, too," said Peter.

Without the proper amount of air and oil inside the forks, the tubes sliding up and down inside each other on both sides of the front wheel would not only take all the smoothness out of the ride, but wear out the tubes as well.

Giff's eyes brightened. "Okay. Come with me, guy. We'll go to Max's, pick up a plug, and check the forks."

Whistling cheerfully, Giff wheeled the bike out of the garage and started it, and Peter climbed on behind him. They rode to Max's Motorbike and Parts Store on Ninth Street, and Giff purchased a spark-plug.

Peter removed the old worn one and screwed the new one in. Then he checked the forks, and, sure enough, both needed about two pounds of air, and also oil. Peter promptly took care of both tasks.

Meanwhile, he had been doing a lot of thinking again, mostly because of the not-too-pleasant atmosphere he had left back there at the MacKenzies'. Mrs. MacKenzie had said that she wanted to have a word with D.C. after the boys left. Peter knew it concerned D.C.'s cool reception toward him — Mrs. MacKenzie had probably talked to D.C. about it by now — but Peter felt there was no way he was going to feel relaxed if he went back there. In fact, he'd probably feel even more uncomfortable than before.

Now, as both of the boys left the parts store and returned to the bike, Giff got on it, but Peter didn't.

"I'm not going back with you, Giff," Peter said evenly. "I'm heading south."

Giff's jaw sagged open. "I don't believe you, Pete," he said, shaking his blond head in wonder. "You know that? I really don't believe you."

7

Giff stared at Peter for several seconds. Before he could speak again, Peter turned and started to walk away. There was no use hanging around any longer.

"So long, Giff. I've got to be going."

"Wait!" cried Giff, running after him. "Think of what you're doing, Pete! Where are you going? You don't know! And you don't know a thing about Fort Myers! You'll be all alone there with no job, no one you know! It just doesn't make any sense, Pete! No sense at all!"

Peter hesitated. Everything Giff said was true. But he couldn't go back with Giff, not when D.C. felt the way she did toward him.

"No, I better go, Giff," he insisted. "I can't go back with you."

"Why? Why can't you?"

"Because I can tell by the look on your sister's face that she isn't happy about me staying there tonight," he said stiffly.

"What?" Giff laughed. "What's *she* got to do with it, anyway? *I* invited you, not D.C. And my mother likes you. She felt sorry for you the minute she got a look at your face and those dirty clothes." Giff was grinning as he said it, and the lightness of the moment transmitted to Peter, bringing a smile to his lips.

"You *will* come and stay, won't you?" Giff said persuasively. "Never mind D.C. Ever since she was stood up by some clown a couple of weeks ago, she's been dead on men. She'll get over it."

Peter looked at him. You must be kidding, Giff, he thought. You know as well as I do that D.C. mistrusts me. She still thinks I'm a bum, a hoodlum, because I rode one of Dex Pasini's bikes. This black eye won't change her mind. Neither will your mother.

Another thought entered his mind, too, and began to nag at him even worse than D.C.'s mistrust of him. Ever since he had run away from the Bentley's he'd been scared. By now they must have notified the police, who'd be searching for him. He was sure of it.

He gnawed worriedly on his lower lip, again torn between the decision whether to go with Giff or head south for Fort Myers.

Giff's eyes bored into his, scrutinizing him as if he were something under a microscope. "Why'd you run away, Pete?" he asked seriously.

Peter weighed the question. "I had to, that's why," he answered soberly.

Giff frowned. "How long were you at the foster home?"

"Six months."

"Only six months? Where were you before that?"

"At The Good Spirit Home. That was in Cross Point, too."

"Want to talk about it?" Giff asked.

Peter thought about it a moment. Maybe it would be a good idea. If there were any doubts about him in Giff's mind, what Peter had to say should clear them up.

Giff relaxed on the saddle of the bike and folded his hands comfortably across his chest. "Have a seat," he offered.

Peter climbed onto the seat behind Giff, rested his feet on the foot pegs, and slowly began to unfold his experiences at The Good Spirit Home, beginning with the death of his parents when he was only about two years old. He told about Dr. Cunningham and the paddle that he had used to whip kids who dared to break the laws of the home.

STEALING, LYING, OR DISOBEYING AUTHORITY SHALL NOT BE TOLERATED IN THE GOOD SPIRIT HOME read the motto engraved on the wood plaque fastened on the wall above the door inside his office. Most of the kids were scared stiff of the doctor. But some of them were bold enough to defy him, just to see what he would do if they got caught.

Some of them had even dared others to pull dirty tricks, as Bugsy Stone had dared Peter a couple of times.

Bugsy was a big kid, a natural leader, who had picked up a following of about five other kids and, subsequently, a name for the group: Bugsy's Angels. And Peter, fearing the consequences if he didn't take on the dare more than he feared the dare, had yielded to them most of the time.

"Bugsy wanted me to steal some money for the

Angels once," Peter explained, remembering the incident as if it were yesterday. "Most of us knew that one of the teachers kept a small box of change in the top drawer of her desk. One day, when I thought no one was looking, I opened the drawer and took the box. There was about eight dollars in it."

"Did you get caught?"

"I did."

"What happened? Dr. Cunningham beat you up with that paddle?"

"He sure did. Besides that, I had to go to my room after supper every night for a week and read *The Rise and Fall of the Third Reich*. Then I had to write summaries on it — and I could hardly understand it!" Peter saw Giff smiling, amused. "Did you read the book?"

Giff nodded. "I did, and I thought it was terrific."

Peter shrugged. "Well, I was only about twelve then, and I didn't. Anyway, the Bentleys came one day, saw me, talked with me, and then with Dr. Cunningham about adopting me. So I went with them — Dr. and Mrs. Bentley and their eighteen-year-old son, Tommy Joe."

He went on to explain his unhappy life with the

Bentleys, particularly about his troubles with Tommy Joe that had culminated in the liquor-drinking episode that had made Peter decide to run away from the place and never go back.

"Oh, wow," Giff said, staring at Peter, incredulous, after Peter was finished. "You sure had your share of troubles, Pete. What about bikes? How come you know so much about them? I know now it wasn't your father who taught you."

"I'm sorry about that," said Peter. "I realize that I've been doing a lot of lying. But what I've told you about The Good Spirit Home and the Bentleys weren't lies," he added hastily, running his hands through his thick, tousled hair.

"I believe you," Giff said, then took a comb out of his pocket and offered it to Peter. "Use it, and keep it," he said. "I've got more."

Peter smiled as he accepted the comb. "Thanks," he said and yanked it though his hair, clearing out the snarls.

When he was done, Giff glanced at Peter's hair with a look of approval. Now all I need is a shower, Peter thought.

"Well," he went on, "one of the maintenance men

at the home, Jim Fairchild, had two bikes, a Kawasaki two-fifty and a Honda four hundred. Both of them big babies. He let me ride with him at first, then let me watch him repair them. He said he used to sell and repair them before he got his job at the home. I took an interest in bikes, and rode and worked on them whenever he'd let me. Finally I got my license, and raced in five or six motos."

"I see." Giff remained quiet awhile, as if he were thinking of something. Finally he looked at Peter, a spark of interest kindled in his blue eyes. "Look, I've got an idea. There's another motocross coming up next Saturday. Why don't you stick around and maybe ride in it? Give yourself another chance against Dex."

Peter looked at him and frowned. What was Giff talking about, anyway? Where was Peter going to get a bike to ride in another moto?

"You seem to forget one important item, Giff," he said. "I don't have a bike. The one I rode today belonged to Dex."

"I know. But if I can get you one, will you stay and ride it in the moto?"

Giff's offer sounded too good to be true. I must be dreaming, Peter thought.

"You're *sure* you can get me a bike to ride?" Peter asked.

Giff lifted his shoulders in a shrug. "More sure than not sure," he said, smiling.

"How am I going to pay my entry fee if you get me a bike?" Peter inquired. "I'm flat broke. Almost, anyway."

Naturally the offer intrigued him. But there was another catch. A big, fat one. Giff said that the moto-cross was going to be run next Saturday. That meant that Peter would have to stick around for a whole week. Would Giff's parents allow it? And what about D.C.? Could she tolerate him for a whole week?

"I'll pay for it," Giff replied, cutting into his worried thoughts. "It's only five bucks. I owe you at least that, anyway, for fixing my bike."

Sure, Peter thought. But what about the meals I'll be sponging off your folks during the week? I'm a growing boy. I eat like a horse, not a bird.

The thoughts tumbled through his mind like crazy, but he didn't want to reveal them to Giff.

"You've got to ask your folks," he said finally. "Maybe they won't want me to stay for a whole week."

Giff rolled his eyes up skyward, then settled them again on Peter. "You're something, you know that?" he said. "Look. An exchange student from Argentina stayed with us for a month once. He couldn't speak a word of English. But we got along fine. And by the time he left us to stay with another family, he could speak well enough to communicate with the least bit of trouble."

Peter's eyebrows arched. "What's that got to do with me?" he asked curiously. "You think I have trouble communicating?"

"No. I'm just using him as an example of what kind of people my parents are," Giff answered resolutely. "They like kids. They love 'em. And . . . who knows?"

He shrugged as he said it, and for a minute Peter wondered what he meant. *Who knows? Maybe they might even consider adopting you.* Is that what ran through his mind?

It was crazy, Peter told himself. Heck, Giff's mother had seen him for only a couple of minutes.

She didn't know a thing about him. She probably had not even realized that he walked with a limp.

And Giff's father hadn't seen him at all.

As for D.C., she'd probably veto the idea with one loud "No!" and not even blink an eye.

"If you must really know, I do have another bike," said Giff, as if it had been a secret he'd wanted to keep to himself until the last minute. "It just needs a lot of fixing."

Peter stared at him. How could two people be so different? he thought. How could Dexter be so cruel to him, and Giff be almost exactly the opposite? Dex would throw him to the dogs because Peter refused to join his gang of crooks, yet Giff was trying his best to help him.

Undecided, he glanced up at the bright blue sky and saw a string of pink clouds in front of the slowly sinking sun. He blinked back tears as he turned and looked at a car moving into a parking space in the adjoining lane.

What should he do? Should he accept Giff's offer, or not? Cypress Corners wasn't really a tremendous distance from Cross Point — only seventy-five miles. Maybe Mr. Fairchild, since he was a motocross enthusiast, would just happen to go to the motocross next Saturday and see Peter there . . . *if* he decided to stay with the MacKenzies and ride in it. What would Mr. Fairchild do? Would he have learned by now that Peter had run away from the Bentleys? Would he approach Peter and try to take him back to them? Peter shuddered at the thought.

"Okay, Pete. You've had your chance," Giff's words cut into his thoughts. "I can't hang around all day. I've got to be going."

Giff put on his helmet, stuck the key into the ignition, and started the engine. He let it idle for a while, and Pete thought it sounded like a purring kitten, pleased at its improvement.

Suddenly he felt the machine move under him, and he quickly wrapped his arms around Giff's waist and hung on tight.

They were heading westward, facing the sun, and Peter had to squint slightly against it. Somehow he was glad he'd been on the bike when Giff had started off. He didn't know what he'd have done if he hadn't been. Probably heading south, he thought.

He was pleased now to be going back with Giff, but a thought began to nag at him again. Try as he might to brush it aside, he couldn't.

Darn it, why should he let D.C. bother him, anyway?

8

They rode to church on Sunday, Mr. MacKenzie driving his blue, two-door Buick and Mrs. MacKenzie sitting beside him. Giff, D.C., and Peter sat in the back seat.

None of the five said a word all the way to church, which was about a mile and a half from their home. Most of the talking had taken place earlier, while they were getting ready to go.

Mrs. MacKenzie had asked Peter if he cared to attend Mass with them, and he'd said yes. He used to go to church every Sunday with the Bentleys. They were also Catholic. He was a Baptist, he said, but he didn't mind going to church with them if they didn't mind it, either. Giff had found an old suit he had outgrown, and it was no trouble for Peter to put on a size 15½ shirt, even though his regular size was 14½.

Last night Mr. MacKenzie had said to Peter that he thought the Bentleys should be notified of Peter's staying with the MacKenzies. It would relieve the Bentleys of worry and assure them that Peter was all right, but that, as of now, he preferred not to go back to them.

"If you think it's the right thing to do," Peter had said.

"It is, Peter," Mrs. MacKenzie had cut in calmly. "Mr. MacKenzie and I talked quite a bit about you and your situation. We're sure it's best for everyone concerned."

So the phone call had been made, much to the Bentleys' appreciation and relief. To Peter's surprise, they didn't mind it one bit that he wanted to stay with the MacKenzies a few days to give him time to think things over. Maybe the MacKenzies would help him come to a right decision on what to do with himself. He'd been afraid that the Bentleys would want him to go back.

In the car he noticed that D.C. had edged up

closer to her brother instead of sitting directly in the middle between them. He had moved as close as he could to the side of the seat, too, leaving a space of about two inches between himself and D.C.

Despite her coolness toward him, he couldn't help noticing how pretty she looked. She was wearing her brown hair back over her left ear and letting it dangle loosely over her right ear, which he thought was funny because it hid one of her white cameo earrings. Her dress was yellow and silky, with short, fluffy sleeves and a narrow white belt. She wore high-heeled shoes, but not the spiky type that made women's ankles wobble when they walked. Hers seemed to be just right. And he liked her perfume.

He wished she'd change her mind about him.

They stopped at a restaurant after church, had breakfast, then returned home. The day was hot and sunny again, and it was about a hundred degrees inside the garage when he got to work on the bike that Giff had told him about.

It was a Muni 125 LC, red-fendered, with twin carburetors. Its worn seat — the stuffing was slightly squeezed out of its sides — was strong evidence that whoever had owned it before had indeed pumped a lot of mileage out of it.

"Dad bought it from a friend of his sometime ago," Giff explained. "The guy needed some ready cash. So really, he didn't invest a heck of a lot of money into it."

"Well, it needs a new plug and a new air box," Peter observed, finding the faults of the bike without much effort. "And the forks need adjustment. I don't know what kind of a rider owned it before, but I don't think he ever checked the air in them. And it needs new shocks, and maybe a transmission overhaul. I can fix a lot of it, but some of the parts will have to be bought." He shook his head. "I don't know, Giff. I'm broke. And maybe your father won't want to put a lot of money into fixing it."

Giff looked at him, grinned, and laid a blunt finger against Pete's chest. "Ease your mind, old buddy. I talked with my father after you went to bed last night. He wants to get that bike running. And I *mean* running. It's been sitting in here too long and is just taking up space, he said. So no matter what it costs to fix it, fix it, he said. He even joked about it. He said that if you're really a good mechanic, you might fix it up so that it'll be better and *faster* than my BLB."

Peter smiled. "That'll be the day," he said.

Peter was able to repair the carburetor and clean the air filter to get the bike running, but it was only in Max Jenkins's bike shop that he was really able to fix the rest of it.

Peter had hated to mention tires, but he didn't have to. It was Giff who saw that new ones were needed and suggested buying them.

All the time Peter worked on the bike, Max, who was either busy with customers or working on a bike himself, kept looking over at him with quiet interest.

When Peter was finished with the bike, he wiped his hands on the grease cloth and asked Max if he would check it over for him. Max seemed astonished at first, but agreed to do it. He went over the bike and scrutinized every detail of Peter's repair job. When he was finished, he shook his head, vastly impressed.

"It's incredible," he declared. "I couldn't have done a better job myself."

"Thanks, Mr. Jenkins," said Peter appreciatively.

When they were ready to leave, Giff started to tell

Max that his father would see him about payment of the bill, but Max raised his hand. "I'm not worried," he said, smiling.

Peter rolled the bike out of the garage and climbed on it, and Giff climbed on behind him.

"Wear this," Giff said, handing Peter his helmet.

Peter put it on, buckled it, then hit the starter. The machine popped off at the first try.

"Is there a hill nearby?" Peter asked as they drove onto the street. "I'd like to give this baby a good test to see how she pulls."

"Yes," replied Giff after thinking a bit. "There's a high, steep pile of dirt that a construction outfit left three or four years ago in a development that they started but never finished. That might do it."

"Might. How do we get there?"

Giff gave directions. Peter maintained a speed of twenty-five miles per hour until they were out of the city limits; then he revved the engine and got it up to fifty, then fifty-five, and held it there.

Peter's pride mounted as he listened to the smooth, rhythmic sound of the engine. Mr. Fairchild would be proud of him, he thought, his heart singing.

The hill was about three miles away in the country, in between an abandoned blacktopped street and a canal. Peter approached it slowly, stopped the bike about twenty feet from its base, and left the engine running.

"Well, what do you think?" Giff asked.

"Wish it were higher," said Peter, looking at the hill with the backdrop of blue sky behind it. "But it'll do."

Giff got off the bike. Smiling, he brushed his wind-blown hair back with his hands. "We'll have to get you a uniform and a helmet," he said.

"And a pair of boots," Peter added. "But maybe there's no need for them. I might not be around long enough to break them in."

Giff looked at him, weighing his words. "Let's cross that bridge when we come to it, okay?"

Peter shrugged. "Sure."

He checked the strap of the helmet Giff let him borrow, revved up the engine, then released the clutch and headed for the hill.

The Muni hit a chunk of dirt and crushed it to bits as the bike stormed up the steep grade, dirt spraying up like machine-gun bullets from its spinning rear wheels.

The going was rough. There was no worn path, no groove into which Peter could line up the bike and sail on. It was virgin territory, every inch of the way.

Two-thirds of the way to the top the front wheel struck another hard lump of dirt and twisted, almost wrenching the handlebars out of Peter's hands. He quickly let up on the gas, straightened the bike out in time, then goosed it again, getting all the power he could out of the Muni.

Seconds later he reached the summit of the hill, cut the engine to idle, and turned to look down at Giff. He was sweating as if he had run up the hill on foot instead of climbed it on the bike. His heart pounded with triumph and joy, as if he had conquered Mount Everest.

Giff waved to him and he waved back, smiling happily behind the plastic shield of the helmet.

Darn! he thought. I know this baby could be a good racer! I just know it could!

They rode home, and both took showers. After a late lunch they sat on the front porch steps, leaning their backs against the tall white pillars, and talked about the Muni's possibilities of coming in among the first five in Saturday's race.

The sound of the front door opening interrupted them. Peter looked up and saw that it was D.C. She had a tray with two tall glasses of ice-cold lemonade on it.

"Thought you hard-working guys might like something cool to drink," she said, bringing it to them.

Peter looked at her and saw her smile. He smiled back, wondering if she was putting it on or if it was really genuine.

9

Peter was hoping that D.C. would remain outside with them and join in their conversation. Maybe she had changed her attitude toward him a little. He had been at the house almost a full day now. D.C. must have been able to see that he wasn't as crummy as she had thought.

Peter and Giff each took a glass of lemonade, Peter glancing up at her after he had taken his. Her brown hair had fallen over the sides of her face, framing her round pink cheeks and brown eyes. Was there something behind that look? he wondered. Was there a hint of forgiveness that she didn't want to put into words just yet?

"Thanks," Peter said, then took a couple of long swallows of the rich-tasting drink. D.C. had taken off her yellow dress and replaced it with a blue

97

blouse and a skirt, he noticed. And instead of the high-heeled shoes, she was wearing toeless pumps.

"You're welcome," she replied pleasantly, and turned to let Giff take his glass from the tray. Then she went back into the house, her long legs lithe and graceful.

For a moment or two Peter felt his heart pound, and put the glass to his lips again to disguise his emotions. He had never been attracted to a girl before as he was attracted to D.C., and he hated to have Giff see him going through this embarrassing strain.

He heard the door close behind D.C., then held the glass on his lap and turned his attention to a tall royal palm across the street upon which a cardinal had just landed. He felt bumbly and awkward. This was silly, he thought. That smile meant nothing. Nothing at all.

Giff's voice broke into Peter's thoughts — gently — as if Giff figured that Peter was immersed in some very personal matter. "I told her about you," Giff said.

Peter stared at him, surprised. "You did? Everything?"

Giff nodded. "Everything. I thought it was the best thing to do. I hope you don't mind."

Peter sat up straighter against the pillar. He looked toward where he had last seen the cardinal. It was gone.

"What did she say?"

Giff shrugged. "She was surprised, and ashamed. She said she'd have to apologize to you." He grinned. "I told you, didn't I?"

Peter grinned. "Yes, you did," he said. But she was out here a few minutes ago, he wanted to say. She had her chance to apologize to him then. Why didn't she? Had she suggested the apology to Giff just to appease him?

Giff finished his drink. "I've just thought of something," he said, holding the empty glass in his hand.

Peter finished his, then looked at Giff, curious.

"How'd you like to ride the Muni on the trail? Just across the canal there's a dirt bike trail where we do a lot of riding. It's got almost enough bumps and curves on it to make it pretty good practice for motos. I've got some work to catch up on in my room. Well, not work, really. I'm a collector."

Peter's eyebrows arched. "What do you collect?"

"Stamps. Coins. Maybe you'd like to see them sometime."

"Sure. Why not?"

It had better be soon, Peter thought. I might not be around here very long.

Giff explained to him how to get to the trail. Then, after Giff and Peter carried their glasses into the house, Peter got the Muni out of the garage, turned left on the street, and cruised down to Georgia Avenue. He turned right, then crossed over a narrow wooden bridge onto a street flanked by a row of tall coconut palms, the ones on the west side leaving the street in deep shadow.

"Look for the dirt bike sign," Giff had said. "It's about a hundred yards up from the bridge, tacked to an electric light pole."

Peter rode slowly, keeping near the edge of the curb, as he watched for the sign.

After riding about a hundred yards he saw the sign and the trail. He turned toward the curb, slowed down, jerked the front end of the bike up onto the curb, then headed down the narrow trail into the woods.

The trail led straight for some twenty yards, then curved to the left, and Peter gave the throttle a gentle twist to goose the engine.

The trail got rougher, and he began to bounce on the seat, feeling the jar on his rear end as if he were sitting on a vibrating machine.

He got to thinking of Giff, of Giff's family, and especially of D.C. If she were given enough time, would she really condescend to apologize to him? Maybe she was shy and saying she was sorry to a person was difficult for her.

The smile she had given him when she brought out the lemonade had some definitive true signs behind it. There was genuine friendliness in it, as there was in her liquid brown eyes.

No matter how she felt about him, he knew how he felt about her. He liked her. Not only her looks and her smooth handling of a bike, but also a gentle softness and warmth he had noticed when she had brought out the tray of lemonade.

But what good was it to keep those feelings inside? And if she wasn't willing to open the door to him first, how could he tell her how he felt toward her?

The sound of a bike shook him out of his reverie. Or was there more than one bike? He wasn't sure. The sound was coming from his left, good and loud, as if the rider or riders were really pouring it on.

The woods here were not as thick as they were near the entranceway, and he was able to see a fairly good distance through them.

Then he saw the bikes. They were on a trail about fifty feet from him, running parallel with the one he was on. There were two of them, one following the other, and both traveling in the opposite direction from which he was traveling.

The lead bike had yellow fenders and a black gas tank. The other had black fenders and a white gas tank. The yellow fenders captured Peter's attention immediately. He'd never forget that bike as long as he lived.

It was Dex Pasini's. The other one was Jess Kutter's.

Peter was quite certain that Dex and Jess had seen him, too. But had they recognized him? He wasn't wearing the same clothes he had worn the day they had met him. Mrs. MacKenzie had thrown them into a hamper to be washed. He was wearing a pair of Giff's pants now, and one of Giff's shirts. It didn't matter that the pants were an inch too long for him; folding up the ends took care of that. The shirt was slightly large for him, too. But, so what?

He remembered the times at The Good Spirit Home when the clothes bought for him did not always fit perfectly either.

The Muni 125 bounced and twisted on the rutted dirt path, jarring every bone in Peter's body as he tried to keep a strong, steady grip on the handlebars, and himself on the seat.

Now and then he glanced back to see whether Dex and Jess had cut off the other trail and onto the one he was on to pursue him, but so far he didn't see them.

An animal — an armadillo — standing directly in his path startled him out of his wits.

"Move!" he shouted, braking and swerving to avoid hitting it.

It moved, all right, but straight into Peter's path. In a desperate effort to dodge it, Peter rammed into a tree. The bike bounced back and tipped over onto its side, spilling him. He rolled over the grass like a top in order to avoid being struck by the bike, and collided into the armadillo.

Fear shot through him as he felt the hard armor of the animal, but the armadillo skittered away and disappeared into the dense brush.

With a pang, Peter saw the bike lying next to the tree, its rear wheel spinning.

He got up, ignoring a pain in his left leg as he scrambled to the machine and shut off its engine. Then he lifted the bike and saw that the front fender was bent.

Anguish assailed him. He looked for other damages and immediately saw that the front headlight was damaged, too.

Heartsick, he thrust the bike up against the tree, collapsed on the grass beside it, and pounded the ground with his clenched fists.

Damn the armadillo! Why did it have to be there then? He closed his eyes tight and rubbed them with his balled fists, then held his breath till the feeling of wanting to cry passed.

Why should this happen to me? he asked himself. What have I done to deserve all this?

Then he heard the sound of the other bikes again. They were approaching from behind him.

Tensed, he waited, and watched for them to appear.

Seconds later they came tearing down the trail, and slowed up abruptly. Dex, Peter saw, was in the lead.

Dex stopped inches away from him, and cut his

engine. "Well, look who's here!" he cried. "Peter Lewinski himself! And with another bike, which, if I'm seeing right, has smashed into a tree! Jess, do you see what I see?"

Jess rode up beside him. He, too, shut off his engine. "Yeah," he muttered dryly.

Peter wondered whether Jess ever said any more than a few words at a time when Dex was around. Probably not.

"Whose bike is that?" Dex went on. Neither he nor Jess had bothered to take off his helmet. "It ain't yours, that's for sure."

"It's Giff MacKenzie's," Peter replied, trying not to be intimidated by anything Dex said or did. Although that sock in the gut that Dex had given him wasn't going to be forgotten in a hurry.

"Oh? Giff MacKenzie's, huh?" Dex said, and Peter thought he could detect a smile of malice behind the blue visor. "I suppose you're staying with him?"

Peter nodded. "With his family," he said.

"For how long?"

"I don't know."

He didn't want to keep talking. Talking would only keep the two from moving on.

105

Dex looked at the Muni, scrutinizing the damage done to the front fender and the headlight. Finally he turned to Jess, who nodded as if a silent message had been exchanged between them. Turning around again, Dex got off his bike, kicked out its rest stand, leaned the bike against it, and walked off into the dense bushes.

Peter could hear him moving around for a minute, then heard the crack of splintered wood. He frowned. What in heck was Dex doing? Peter felt his heart pound as he glanced at Jess and saw a sly, amused grin spread over his face through the visor.

Then Dex reappeared, carrying a branch about four feet long and three inches thick. Peter stared at him, terror seizing him as he wondered what Dex intended to do with the club.

His eyes were glazed with fear as he sprang to his feet and backed away.

"What do you think you're going to do with that?" he cried, taking another step back. "You gone wacky?"

A chuckle issued from behind the visor. Then Dex stopped in front of Giff's bike, raised the club high over his head, and brought it down hard against the right-side suspension fork.

The resounding blow bent the tube almost up against the front wheel and split the branch.

"You rat!" Peter shouted, and dove at Dex, hoping to get at him before he could wield the broken club again.

But Dex, as if he had expected Peter to make just such a move, sprang away, ready to swing the club at him.

"Come on, jerk," Dex challenged him, "and I'll let you have it, too."

Peter stood, staring grimly into the glittering eyes that stared back at him. He saw now that Jess was also off his bike and had it resting on its stand while he stood nearby, ready to jump on Peter.

Dex waited a few seconds, then turned and heaved the broken branch into the woods, where it struck a tree and dropped to the ground. He picked up the other piece of it and flung that away, too. Then he went to his bike, kicked up the rest stand, and started it.

Jess followed suit. In a minute both of them were gone, headed back in the direction from which they had come.

Peter listened to their roaring engines subsiding

in the distance, then surveyed the damages done to the Muni. His throat burned, and he blinked back tears as he approached the machine and checked it to see if the front suspension fork was touching the tire or the spokes. Both tongs were bent, Peter observed, but still cleared the tire and spokes. The tubes would not be sliding freely up and down, and the bike would ride rough. The fork, therefore, would require straightening out. More likely, a new replacement would be needed.

Sick with despair, Peter lifted the bike upright, turned it around to face the direction of the street, and got back on it. What was Giff going to say when he saw the damage? Would he have it repaired, regardless of the cost? Or would he be so sore that he'd change his mind about Peter's racing in Saturday's motocross?

Clamping his lips hard together, Peter started the bike and rode ahead, wishing now that he had not listened to Giff. He should have gone on to Fort Myers as he had planned to do in the first place.

10

It was D.C. who first saw him as he entered the kitchen door. Her eyes lowered immediately to his pants, where smudges of dirt covered his knees and his right thigh.

"What in the world happened to you?" she said, incredulous. "You look like you were in a smashup."

"I was," he said, closing the door behind him. "Is Giff still in his room?"

"I think so. But —"

"I tried to keep from running over a stupid armadillo," he started to explain. "Instead, I ran into him and lost control of the bike. It was dumb."

Her eyebrows arched. "Armadillo?"

"Right. Dumb," he repeated.

"If you say so," she said, and turned slowly around and walked away.

He watched her back a minute and had it on the tip of his tongue to explain to her why he had run into the stupid animal, why he had accelerated the bike, causing him to run into it. But he was afraid it would sound like a poor excuse to her. And anyway, why should she care?

He wiped his shoes off on the mat and went upstairs. The door to Giff's room was closed.

He knocked on it.

"Come in," said Giff's voice.

Peter opened the door and stepped into the room. Giff turned away from his desk, looked at Peter, then at the dirt smudges on his pants.

"Oh, no!" he exclaimed. "What happened, Pete? You get into an accident?"

Peter sat down on the edge of the bed and told him, starting from the minute he had heard the sound of the two bikes.

Giff listened intently, his eyes darkening at the mention of Dex's and Jess's names. When Peter was finished he got up, and Peter could see the book of stamps on the desk, the loose stamps that lay beside it. Giff must have thousands of them, he thought.

"Damn his guts," Giff swore as he brushed past Peter and out of the door.

Peter got up and followed him down the stairs and outside to the driveway, where he had left the Muni parked on its kick stand. Giff drew up beside it, looked at its bent fender and fork and damaged headlight, then walked around it, looking for other signs of damage.

"That's it," said Peter. "And some scratches. You want to call the cops?" The words had barely left his mouth when he realized what that might mean. "I don't want to press charges."

"Right. So forget the cops. We'll fix it up, Pete. You're going to ride her in Saturday's moto. Okay?"

A smile spread from ear to ear on Peter's face. He hadn't expected Giff to say that.

"Okay!" he cried, jubilant.

Giff's insurance on the Muni, covering collision, took care of most of the repair that Giff had to spend on it.

Peter fixed the bike himself, buying the needed parts from Max's Motorbike and Parts Store. It took him till Wednesday evening to finish it. Then, on Thursday morning, he and Giff rode out to the Bumble Bee Speedway to try out the Muni.

D.C. went with them, driving her blue YZ 125 Yamaha and wearing her bright-red satiny suit and polished leather boots.

Peter had secretly wished that she would go along with them, but had not said anything because, deep inside, he was too shy. But Giff had invited her, and she had glanced at Peter and said she'd be glad to go if he didn't mind. Mind? Was she crazy? Of course he didn't mind. Anyway, she had quickly gotten into her gear, hopped onto her bike, and ridden along.

There was a fee to get on the track, and Giff paid it for all three of them.

They lined up at the starting line as they would in a real race. Then Giff took off first, and Peter and D.C. a second later. They zoomed up the hill, D.C. gaining a quick lead and reaching the summit first.

She was ahead by about five lengths by the time Peter and Giff were at the bottom of the hill, the long, level stretch straight ahead of them. Then Giff streaked ahead of Peter, and Peter gunned it, too, catching up to him, then slowly edging past him.

He could see D.C. rounding the curve ahead and then executing the jump gracefully. He and Giff came upon the jump-hill simultaneously, and for a split second he and the bike were airborne, his body — except for his hands gripping the handle-bars — entirely free of the bike.

The rear wheel of the Muni hit the ground first, and a second later the front wheel hit the ground, too. Peter landed hard on the seat and bounced up again as the wheels rolled and bounded and thundered down the track. The suspension forks were getting a workout that they had not had, Peter was sure, in a long time.

The three of them completed a run around the 1.3-mile track, no one pressing his or her machine to its limit, but all riding as if to acquaint themselves again with the curves, the berms, and the jump-hills.

Peter was pleased with the performance of the Muni, and by the third time he'd circled the track he gunned the engine to really see what the machine could do.

He passed D.C. going down the stretch after making the sharp turn at the finish line, and couldn't help smiling when he saw her head turn his way.

He was about two lengths ahead of her when, from the corner of his eye, he saw her creeping back up beside him. He slowed briefly as he approached the jump-hill. There was no use running any risks now by taking the hill as fast as the Muni could go, he thought. But D.C. seemed to be oblivious to risks. She zipped by him just as they reached the peak, landed before he did, and was back in the lead.

He tried to catch up to her again, but during the next two laps she didn't relinquish her lead to him by more than the length of a bike, and at times, she even led him by about three lengths.

He was surprised, and amused, by her valiant driving. Never before had he seen a girl drive a bike as well as she. He knew now that she was indeed a competitor, a factor he had scarcely considered before.

They ran a few more laps; then Giff slowed down at the finish line, pulled up to the side, and stopped. D.C. slowed up and stopped beside him, and Peter pulled up beside her.

"Well," Giff said as he looked at Peter through his visor, "how does the baby run?"

"Fine. I think I'll check the nuts and bolts when

we get back, though. The rough drive might've loosened them up."

Peter glanced at D.C. and saw that the legs of her satiny crimson uniform were covered with dirt. He smiled and wondered if she'd wash the uniform before she'd trial-run, or race, the Yamaha again.

"Peter?"

He looked up at her eyes, which he was scarcely able to see through the visor of her helmet. "Yes?"

"I'm sorry about the way I acted toward you in the beginning. I was dumb. Giff told me everything. I hope you'll forgive me."

Her voice was soft, sincere. Peter knew she meant every word. His heart warmed, and began to pound. "There's nothing to forgive, D.C.," he said, his voice catching in his throat for a second. "But I'm glad. Thanks."

He turned and looked at Giff. Giff smiled at him and winked. "Hey, think the Muni will be set to go Saturday?" Giff asked, his voice booming.

Peter grinned. "I guarantee it!" he cried, jubilant.

"Great!" Then Giff goosed the engine of his bike gently and started to lead the way back toward home. D.C. followed, riding up close beside him, and Peter rode up next to her. Somehow, Peter thought without glancing again at her, even a dirty uniform looked good on her.

Back at the garage he found that some of the nuts and bolts on the Muni had loosened slightly from the hard, jarring ride, and he tightened them.

After lunch they washed, cleaned, and polished their bikes, then gassed them up at the local gas station.

It was about three o'clock when Peter, wishing he could do something around the place to help pay for his room and board, saw that the lawn could stand a mowing. Without mentioning it to Giff, or to Mrs. MacKenzie for that matter, he went out, got the lawnmower out of the utility building behind the garage, filled it with gasoline from a two-gallon metal container, and proceeded to mow the lawn.

The sun was lost behind a gray, overcast sky, and the day was hot and humid, causing the shirt to stick to his back. He took it off and laid it over a corner post of the porch steps, then continued to mow the lawn till he was finished. It wasn't a very big lawn, and he didn't think he had spent more than fifteen or twenty minutes mowing it.

What else could he do? He just couldn't sit around all the time. He liked to draw cartoons, but he wouldn't look busy sitting in the living room, drawing crazy pictures. Doing that was fun, not work.

He gazed at the shrubbery and at the sea grapes that grew along the back fence with a bed of huge, brown, dried leaves lying beneath them. Though the MacKenzies kept a clean backyard — and front yard, too — it looked as if the fallen leaves had gotten ahead of them.

He went back to the utility shed, carried out one of the two garbage cans sitting in there, and piled the dried leaves into it. Then he stood back, studied the growth of sea grapes, and saw where he could improve their looks by a snip here and a snip there. Whistling softly through his teeth, he ran back to the shed, found a pair of shrubbery clippers, and went to work.

He didn't stop with the sea grapes. He trimmed the hibiscus plant, too, and some of the other plants that he couldn't identify by name. He had done the same for the Bentleys, except that he found doing the job here was much easier.

Why had he found it so hard to do it for them and

not for the MacKenzies? he thought. Why had he always felt that he had to *ask* the Bentleys if he could trim their plants? *Ask* if he could mow their lawn? Yet feel free to go ahead and do those things here without asking?

He was almost done when he heard a car drive up into the driveway and recognized the rasping sound of Mr. MacKenzie's Buick. Maybe he'd let me work on it someday, Peter thought. Smooth it up for him.

He was still out there when he heard the back door open and close and heard Mr. MacKenzie's voice addressing him. He turned from the plant he was working on and saw the tall, broad-shouldered man come down the steps and head toward him.

He must be around 220 pounds, Peter guessed, and hardly any of it fat. He jogged every morning before breakfast — three miles down alongside the canal, three miles back — and played golf twice a week. "If he didn't do those things he'd go up to two-fifty," Giff had said.

"Hi, Peter," Mr. MacKenzie greeted him, tiny wrinkles forming at the corners of his dark brown eyes as he smiled. "How are you doing?"

"Just fine, sir, I think," replied Peter.

The man's black eyebrows stood out like rolled-up shades as he bit into an apple he was holding in his left hand. Suddenly he made a motion with his other hand, and Peter saw something come floating through the air at him.

"Catch," Mr. MacKenzie said.

It was another apple. Peter dropped the clippers and caught the apple, a large, shiny red one.

"Thanks," he said, and sank his teeth into its sweet, juicy pulp.

"Did a nice job," Mr. MacKenzie observed, looking over the plants that Peter had trimmed. "Do you like that kind of work?"

Peter shrugged. "I don't mind it. I did a lot of it for the Bentleys."

"They appreciated it, I'm sure."

"I suppose they did," said Peter.

"Didn't they say so?"

"Once."

"Well . . ." Mr. MacKenzie smiled. "Once is better than never."

He took another bite of the apple, looked at it

while he chewed, then shot his eyes back to Peter. "You don't aim to go back to them?"

"No, I don't." Peter didn't flinch a bit from Mr. MacKenzie's cool, appraising gaze.

"You're sure?"

"I could never go back there, Mr. MacKenzie," Peter replied seriously. "Not as long as their son lives with them, anyway."

"What about them? Mr. and Mrs. Bentley?"

Peter shrugged. "They're okay."

"Did you get very close to them? I mean — did you get to like them very much, and did they like you?"

Peter hesitated. The big man was looking at him intently, waiting for him to answer. "I don't know," he said. "I'm not sure about that."

Mr. MacKenzie's face seemed to relax. He looked at the apple in his hand again, took another bite of it, then glanced around once more at the work Peter had done.

"Look, Peter," he said calmly, "it seems to me that you've done plenty for one day. Why don't you clean up now and come into the house? Okay?"

"Okay." He was nearly finished anyway, he thought. He'd do the rest tomorrow.

11

Nobody seemed surprised when the name of the winner of the first twenty-minute heat, run Saturday at the Bumble Bee Speedway, was announced.

Dex Pasini had won it by four bike lengths.

"Well, he did it again," D.C. said, taking off her helmet and wiping her sweating forehead with the palm of her hand. Then she shook her head, letting her hair cascade down over her shoulders, where the sunlight flashed onto it.

"Yeah. But he won't always be so lucky," said Peter, hanging his orange helmet over a handlebar of the Muni and wiping his own sweating face with a handkerchief. He was hot and uncomfortable under the orange uniform that Giff had let him borrow, even after having unzipped it. And his feet seemed to be burning inside the short leather boots in spite of the sweat socks. But he wasn't going to complain. Being with the MacKenzies was paradise compared with The Good Spirit Home or the Bentleys, or even living in Fort Myers, where he'd be a total stranger.

He had finished in fifth place in the heat, and D.C. in sixth. Giff, who had finished in third place, now stood beside his bike, mopping his face and forehead with a red, oversized handkerchief.

"Maybe not," Giff said. "But how long is it going to be before somebody breaks his lucky streak?"

Peter shrugged. "Who knows? Maybe it'll happen in the next heat," he replied, grinning.

He didn't want to say what he thought — because Giff and D.C. might think he was too cocksure if he did — but he felt that he had a good chance himself of beating Dex. Twice during the heat he had come within two bike lengths of Dex, only to lose ground — once at a sharp turn, the second time at a jump-hill. The next heat could be a different ride altogether.

The three of them strode over to the concession

stand, where they each had a Coke while they waited for the second heat to start.

Promptly at two o'clock, the gun went off and the second heat was on.

A green-tanked Husky 125 bolted over the dropped gate first. Giff was second and Dex third, followed by the rest of the fifteen riders. Four of the original nineteen had to drop out for various reasons — mainly engine troubles.

Only one biker failed to make the first hill on the initial try. He lost his balance and fell over backwards, miraculously escaping being hit by another bike. By the time he got up, scrambled to his vehicle, and got it moving again, he was about fifty yards behind the next rider.

Peter, ninth behind the leader — the Husky 125 — saw the green-tanked machine execute the first jump-hill with the ease of a bird. Giff was next, and then Dex. A Derbi 125, No. 38, was fourth; Jess Kutter, No. 123, was fifth. D.C. was seventh.

In seconds Peter was approaching the jump-hill, too. Then he was soaring over it, his hands steel-tight on the handlebars as he stood tense and anxious during that brief flight in midair till the wheels hit.

His rear end came down and made contact with the seat. He held on, thoroughly in control, and in seconds had the bike breezing over the track again.

The washboard ride came up next, jarring every bone in his body, and he was thankful for a few moments of respite when the track smoothed out so that he could find a line and stay on it, even if it was for only a short while.

The first lap ended with a few changes in the front runners. Dex was now in the lead, the Husky was second, and the Derbi was third. Peter was still ninth or tenth, he wasn't sure which. By the third lap he gave up trying to keep track of his position. He wasn't even sure who was leading now. He was just interested in passing the bike in front of him, and then the one in front of that.

But by the end of ten minutes, he saw that he was sixth behind the leader. They were all bunched up in front of him. On the previous lap he had passed D.C. and figured that she was now in about seventh place. Or even farther back if she wasn't able to hold it.

Twice during the next four minutes Peter lost ground and fell back into eighth position, and didn't see D.C. But going into the final seconds he was again near the front of the pack. Dex was leading; No. 101 was in second position, Giff in third, Jess in fourth, and Peter in fifth.

Peter crept ahead, knowing it would feel good to let Jess Kutter see *his* tail for awhile. He had been looking at Jess's long enough.

He inched forward — only a few seconds were left now — and ahead of them a jump-hill was coming up fast.

Then he was ahead of Jess and widening the gap between them. Eat my dust for a change, Jess, ol' kid! he cried exultantly to himself.

Then, out of the corner of his left eye, Peter saw the front wheel of Jess's bike turn toward him. Surprised, Peter turned to get a better view of Jess's bike and saw that it *was* headed toward him.

A rush of panic sent chills down his spine. What did Jess think he was doing?

Peter reverted his attention back to the track

ahead, turned the wheel of his bike slightly, and goosed the engine to demand more speed out of the Muni. But Jess was too close to him, and suddenly the front wheel of his bike touched the back fender of Peter's.

"Move, baby! Move!" Peter cried.

He felt the bump again. Only this time it was harder, hard enough to thrust the rear of Peter's bike slightly to one side and off its line.

Peter twisted the throttle, trying to slow his bike and bring it back under control. He shot his legs out to help keep his balance, and that of the bike, but already the front wheel had skidded to the right. It was too late.

The bike rolled over, and he went with it, letting go of the handlebars as he lost control of the bike.

He rolled over and over, praying that he wouldn't be struck by an oncoming bike, or even by his own.

He wasn't, and when he came to a stop, he quickly scrambled to his feet, finding himself almost up against the fence that lined the right side of the track. His bike lay a few feet away from him, its front wheel still spinning, its rear wheel turning slowly, knobbies clawing at the dirt.

The other bikers were speeding by it, keeping to the left of it, a couple of them missing it only by inches. Peter sprang toward it, lifted it to its wheels, then glanced toward the finish line.

Despair welled up in him. Already most of the riders had streaked across it, the checkered flag whipping down as each one sailed by.

"Keep going! Keep going!" someone shouted to him from behind the fence. Others joined in, encouraging him to ride on.

What's the use? he thought. What's the difference whether I finish the race now or not? I'm way behind, thanks to that punk Jess Kutter.

But he rode the bike ahead and across the finish line, and came in twelfth place despite the seconds he had lost in the accident.

He looked around for Jess and saw him some distance away on the track, sitting on his bike. Next to him was Dex, straddling his. Both were looking back at him; then they turned away when they saw him looking at them.

Peter's blood boiled. Smirk, you rats! he thought. One of these days I'll get even with you for this!

But when? When would he be able to avenge

himself? His stay with the MacKenzies was indefinite. Probably they'd keep him another week at the most. If they did, he'd have his chance. It would have to be on the track. That was the only place the showdown could be held.

Giff and D.C. came running up to him as he got off his bike and began brushing the dirt off his suit. There was a tear in the material of his right elbow, and he felt a slight burning pain there now that he hadn't felt before.

"Peter! You okay?" Giff cried.

"Yeah, I'm okay," he said.

"I'm so sorry," said D.C., looking at him plaintively. "You could've come in ahead of Kutter. I'm sure you would have."

He looked at her and realized that she — and probably no one else — had seen Jess Kutter bump deliberately into him. It was most important for the track marshal to have seen the infraction, in which case Jess would be disqualified. But obviously even he had not seen it, or an announcement would have been made by now.

"Yeah. I suppose," he said, holding the smoldering anger deep down inside him.

The announcement of the winners started to come over the public address system. "Ladies and gentlemen, winner of the second heat, number forty-four, Dexter Pasini!"

A roar exploded from the fans, and died as the voice continued. "In second place, number one-oh-one, Dave Melburg!"

Another roar resounded. Number 101, Peter remembered, was a silver-tanked, blue-fendered Yamaha.

The Derbi 125 came in third; Giff fourth; Jess Kutter fifth. D.C. came in eighth.

Only the first four winners picked up trophies, but the first eleven each picked up points. For his first-place victory in both heats Dex Pasini earned forty points — twenty points from each heat — to add to his total of sixty-one. Giff earned nine points for having come in third in the first heat, and eight for having came in fourth in the second heat, bringing his total up from forty to fifty-seven.

Not a good day's run for him, Peter thought as he contemplated how eager Giff had been to beat Dex for a change.

He said nothing about the infraction to anyone till

D.C. brought up his mishap again at the dinner table. She was helping her mother serve a steaming-hot casserole when she looked at Peter and met his eyes. "Peter, I saw Jess riding pretty close to you just before the race finished," she said and paused, frowning. "The next thing I saw was your bike going out of control."

He nodded. "That's right."

"Did he bump into you?"

He shrugged. Would she believe him if he told her? Would anyone believe him?

"Did he?" she repeated.

"Yes, he did. But I guess no one noticed. Not even the track marshal."

"Who should have," D.C. said. Her lips pressed together defiantly, and her eyes flashed. "I got to thinking about that later," she said. "Knowing Kutter, I *knew* he must have done something. He and Dex are like two peas in a pod. I wouldn't trust either one of them as far as I could throw a bull."

"There'll be a race coming up Wednesday at Sunway," Giff intervened. "Next time, keep far enough ahead of him so that he won't have a chance to pull anything dirty."

"All right, let's cut out the character smudging right now," Mrs. MacKenzie said. "Remember the saying 'He who points a finger at someone points three at himself.'"

"Uh-oh, the wise old sage herself," D.C. said, and smiled. "Forgive us for pointing, Mom."

"Shush up now, and talk later," her mother said, and reached over for Peter's plate.

He handed it to her, feeling his appetite whetted as he watched her ladle steaming beef tips, noodles, and stewed tomatoes onto his dish.

We got a call last night from Dr. Bentley, Peter," Mr. MacKenzie said to him at breakfast on Monday morning. "He and his wife want to know what we intend to do with you."

Peter had just finished eating. He figured that Mr. MacKenzie had waited for him to finish his breakfast before he mentioned the call because of how it might affect him.

He'd been thinking a lot about the Bentleys, wondering what *they* intended to do if he and the MacKenzies didn't come to a decision soon. Most of yesterday was a drag because he couldn't stop thinking about what was going to happen to him.

He wiped his mouth with a napkin, stared at the empty bowl in front of him, and began to feel a gnawing sensation in the pit of his stomach, a feeling that usually came to him whenever he got to thinking about the Bentleys and his running away from their home.

"I told him that we weren't quite sure yet," Mr. MacKenzie said. "I asked him to give us another week."

A fly landed on the edge of the bowl and began to rub its front legs together. Peter swiped at it, and it flew away.

"After Peter stays with us another week, what then, Dad?" D.C. asked, curious. "Are you going to ask the Bentleys to come and take him back?"

"That's not for us to say right now, D.C.," said her father. "Anyway, you know that Peter doesn't want to go back and live with them." He paused. "You still determined on that stand, Peter?"

Peter glanced at him, then turned his attention back to the bowl again as if it had suddenly produced an overwhelming fascination for him. "Yes," he said stiffly.

"Let's not embarrass Peter by talking about that now," Mrs. MacKenzie intervened politely. "There is one thing we should say to you, though, Peter. The Bentleys would like to have you back. I talked with

Mrs. Bentley last night. She says she and her husband both want you to come back to them. She promised that things will be different. What those things are, she didn't say. But I feel that we should let you know what she said."

"Thank you," he said.

Things would be different? What things? She was still working, wasn't she? She would have mentioned it if she weren't. And her husband was still doctoring, wasn't he? He wasn't going to cut his hours just to accommodate Peter. It was their absence from home that had made life so lonely for him. That and their son's unbearable behavior.

He couldn't go back there. He *wouldn't* go back there. He just had to wait and see what the Mac-Kenzies decided to do with him. If they wanted him to stay, he would. Oh, God, wouldn't that be great, he thought. I'd be in a real good home at last, with a family that's tops.

What about D.C.? he asked himself. Would she get to like him better? Well, the ice seemed to have melted between them. She was talking to him more than she had during his first few days of living with them. And she had seen — had thought she had, anyway — Jess Kutter bumping into him at the motocross. Didn't that mean that she was taking an interest in him, in what he was doing? At least she was becoming more aware of his presence. That alone meant a lot.

Mr. MacKenzie brought up the question about school. It was the first time the subject was mentioned. Peter said that he was a junior in high school. He confessed that his grades in his sophomore year weren't anything he could brag about, but at least they were good enough to get him into the eleventh grade.

"Is there something you would like to do after you graduate?" Mrs. MacKenzie asked him. "I know it's too soon to make a decision yet, but have you thought of any career at all?"

"Oh, Mom," Giff said, turning to look at her. "He's only sixteen. *My* age. And *I* haven't figured out what I'd like to do yet."

"Neither have I," said D.C. "Except, well, maybe an airline stewardess."

"Dear, you haven't even been up in an airplane yet," her mother declared, flashing a surprised smile.

"I know that, Mother," D.C. replied emphatically.

"All I'm trying to say is that I know what I'd like to do when I'm out of school."

"I'm sorry. I guess I was too abrupt," said her mother apologetically. "Forgive me, dear. Anyway, I had addressed the question to Peter."

Peter smiled and cleared his throat. "No, I haven't thought of what I'd like to do," he said.

Mrs. MacKenzie shrugged. "Well, like Gifford said —"

"I like to draw, though," Peter cut in.

"Oh?" Mrs. MacKenzie's eyes lighted up. "What do you like to draw, Peter?"

"Cartoons."

"Cartoons?" Her eyebrows arched.

"Hey, that's great!" Giff cried. "That's terrific!"

"Some cartoonists become very rich," D.C. cut in, looking wide-eyed at him, as if she were suddenly seeing a new and different person.

Peter smiled. "Rich? Me? I might be lucky to even make a living at it."

"Don't cut yourself short, Peter," Mr. MacKenzie said quietly. "If you have the talent and like doing it, you could do very well."

He went to bed that night thinking of what Mr.

MacKenzie had said, and of becoming a famous cartoonist. Maybe he'd have a comic strip syndicated in a hundred newspapers someday, he thought. Maybe five hundred.

They left right after dinner on Wednesday evening for the Sunway Racetrack some thirty-five miles south of Cypress Corners. Mr. MacKenzie had borrowed a Chevy pickup from a neighbor to haul the three bikes on it, plus a couple of spare tires and a few sparkplugs — just in case.

Sunway was a small track, less than a mile from start to finish — 0.8 mile to be exact — and rough. Giff and D.C. had raced on it several times, they said, and had fared better there than on the Bumble Bee Speedway, but that was because it didn't attract the better, faster riders that Bumble Bee did.

Twice Giff had come in first place, and D.C. once, the only time, she told Peter, that she had ever come in first place. Could lightning strike again? There it might, she'd said optimistically, the corners of her eyes crinkling up with hope.

Thirteen riders competed — including three whom Peter dreaded to see there: Dex Pasini, Jess Kutter, and Bill Rocco. All three had their own same bikes: Dex his Corella, Jess his Yamaha, and Bill his Fitz RK.

There was no high hill to climb to knock off the fledglings as there was at the Bumble Bee Speedway, but the choppy track took its toll nevertheless. A green Suzuki and a black Honda careened into each other going around a hairpin curve halfway around the track, and it was mainly the choppy track that was the cause. Giff had warned Peter about it before the moto had started, but he didn't realize how really treacherous the curve was until he had gone over it a couple of times.

There were two heats, twenty laps in each, with trophies going to the first-place winner and the two runners-up. Peter wasn't as keen about winning any of the three top spots as he was about actually participating in the moto. It kept him busy, and his mind free of worries. He'd be in a moto every day if it were possible.

He wasn't surprised that one of the three cohorts he had hoped not to see at the moto started to give him a bad time. This time it was Bill Rocco.

Rocco's Fitz RK was a German make with silver-gray fenders higher off the wheels than most

American- or Japanese-made bikes. It was air-cooled and quick as a cat. Peter noticed its maneuverability when it headed into the hairpin curve just ahead of him, then shot directly into his path as he started to pass by it going down a short stretch. He almost rammed into the Fitz's tail and had to cut his speed to avoid a collision.

Thereafter, for the next four laps, he and Rocco were hub to hub most of the time. On the thirteenth lap they were cutting another sharp curve, and were again hub to hub — their legs off the pegs to help balance their bikes — when Rocco, riding on the inside, caught Peter's ankle with his foot and gave it a violent jerk.

Peter lurched, causing his Muni to twist crazily to the right, heading for sure destruction into a fence unless he could bring the bike back into line without causing it to lose its balance.

Paralysis gripped him for a brief instant as he stared at the fence. It was about four feet high, with spectators standing on the other side of it, their eyes wide and intent on the scene that was happening before them.

Quickly he rose from the seat and leaned over to

the left — giving the handlebars as much twist as he dared without risking letting the bike go into a dangerous skid — and just briefly grazed the fence.

Then he was clear of it and once again speeding down the track. Rocco was some twenty feet ahead of him now. Peter watched him shooting down the straightaway and tried to swallow the anger that had welled up in him. Were those three guys — Dex, Jess, and Bill — taking turns harassing him?

Then it was over. Peter crossed the finish line a poor ninth. Dex came in first, D.C. second, a Honda third, and a Suzuki fourth. Giff had not been able to finish. His rear tire had blown on the eleventh lap, forcing him out of the race.

An announcement came over the public address system that Peter paid no attention to until he saw D.C. turn and stare wide-eyed at him. Then her face lit up in a broad, happy smile, and she began to jump and wave with joy. Peter gave his full attention to the announcement then, and his heart quickened as he heard his name.

". . . causing Peter Lewinski to lose control of his bike, thereby endangering Lewinski and other bikers on the track. The infraction, according to the judgment of the race director, disqualifies William Rocco in the first heat, and also in the second."

"He *did* see it!" Peter exclaimed, incredulous, and gazed around for Rocco to see what his reaction was to the announcement.

"Yes, he did!" D.C. declared. She grabbed Peter's arm and clutched it tightly. Her eyes were big and round. "Peter! Didn't you get hurt? No *bruises?*"

He shrugged. "A little hurt here and there. But not much."

"I can't believe that . . . that punk," she said, looking around.

"Believe it," said her brother. "They're three of a kind."

"Where are they?" D.C. asked. "I'd like to see Rocco's face."

"You can't. Not yet, anyway," said Giff softly. "He's standing there at the concession stand with his back to us. Dex and Jess are next to him."

Peter and D.C. saw them. Dex and Jess were leaning against the stand, holding cans of soft drink. Dex was peering directly at Peter. Peter gazed back at him, unflinching.

"Just keep an eye on him during the next heat,"

Giff advised quietly. "He's smarter at dirty tricks than Jess and Bill are put together."

"I doubt that he'll try anything foolish, though," said D.C. skeptically. "Jess might, but not Dex. He won the first heat. He'll want to make sure he wins the second one, too."

But the second heat turned out to be a disaster for all three of them — Giff, D.C., and Peter. Giff had another blown tire, D.C.'s Yamaha a blown gasket, and Peter's Muni conked out five minutes before the race ended. Carburetor trouble, Peter discovered when he checked the machine.

There was little said during their ride home, and most of it was about the upcoming motocross at the Bumble Bee Speedway on Saturday.

"You guys will have to get that engine fixed up for me before then, that's for sure," D.C. declared. "I can't miss that one. They're giving away goodies."

"Oh? Like what?" Peter asked.

"Like tires, jackets, and helmets," Giff replied.

Fine, thought Peter. I'd settle for any one of them. But what I'd *really* like to do is beat Dex, who was still on his lucky streak. That, mused Peter, would be the frosting on the cake.

13

Sleep came hard to Peter that night. He tossed from one side of the bed to the other, wondering if the MacKenzies liked him enough to keep him or not.

He had hoped that something about it would have been said at the dinner table or later on in the evening. But not a word of it was brought up.

The next morning he worked on D.C.'s bike. He took the engine apart while Giff rode his BLB to Max's parts store and purchased a new gasket.

He put the gasket on, then checked the YA 125 Yamaha as thoroughly as if it were the bike *he* was going to race in the motocross Saturday. Several minor adjustments were required: the points, a tiny leak in the gas line, some loose spokes in both wheels.

When he was finished and had double-checked the bike by taking it out on a ride, giving it his stamp of approval, D.C. hand-washed it and then polished it to a bright, glistening sheen.

"Hey, buddy, you're going to give that baby of mine that same TLC treatment, aren't you?" Giff asked Peter, a broad smile on his face.

"Why not?" he said, and then went as thoroughly over Giff's bike as he had D.C.'s. What a beauty, he thought as he looked over its liquid-cooled engine, the plastic fuel tank, the 38-mm Frabozzi suspension forks in front, the Pinter gas shocks in back. The radiator was under the fuel tank, mounted to a pair of backbone tubes less than seven inches from the top of the cylinder head.

"Did you know it could kick-start while it's in gear?" Giff said proudly. "I don't often start it that way, but it's no problem."

"No. I didn't know that," Peter admitted. "You have a killer here, Giff. You really have. Know what? I wish it was mine."

"Sorry, Pete. But when it comes to that BLB, I'm a stinker. I can't help it. You can ride it as often as you wish. But own it? Never."

Peter laughed. "I know what you mean. I'd feel the same way."

He checked the carburetion, which was perfect. It hadn't loaded up a bit. He had to remove the seat to check the filter and found that it, too, wasn't bad. He tapped it against the cement floor a few times anyway, to knock out the thimbleful of tiny particles of dirt that had accumulated in it.

He could find nothing else that needed even a minor turn or twist, and rode the bike around a couple of blocks to make sure.

"I don't know," he said as he rode up onto the floor of the garage and shut off the engine. "Looks to me like you and D.C. have a couple of winners here, Giff."

Giff smiled. "Get the Muni fixed up and we'll have three of them," he said cheerfully.

Peter got off the BLB, and Giff rolled it over to the side, where he started at it with soap and water. Peter went over to the Muni, looked at the dirt packed onto its fenders, knobbies, and other parts of it, and began to wipe them off with a soft brush and a cloth. Then he checked the bike's working parts and found that they could use a little more transmission oil and air in the tires. The points needed adjustment, too.

It took an hour for him to put it into the shape he felt could make it compete with the best and fastest of bikes, then finished the job with a hand-wash and polish.

At noon Giff got a call from Jay Wallace of Wallace's Nursery, asking him if he'd like to help him out on Friday in planting trees and shrubbery at the new mall that was being built just outside of Cypress Corners.

Giff not only accepted the job, but got one for Peter, too. He said that every once in a while, since last summer when he had worked at the nursery, Mr. Wallace would give him a call when he needed extra help on a job. The opportunity to earn a few dollars sounded good to Peter, who went to bed that night wondering what he'd do with the money.

He'd give it to Giff, he decided. Or to Mrs. MacKenzie. After all, look what they had done for him during these two weeks that he'd been with them.

But on Friday evening, after the work was done

and Mr. Wallace paid them in cash, Giff refused to accept the money from Peter.

"You crazy?" he said, staring at Peter as if he were insulted. "It's yours. You earned it. You owe me nothing."

Later, when Peter offered to give it to Giff's mother, she refused to accept it, too.

"Keep it," she told him. "You'll find use for it, don't worry."

He couldn't believe it. They were so good to him.

That night he began to think of buying a gift for them. He had to do something for them to show his appreciation. And they *had* to accept a gift if he got it.

But what could he buy?

"You'll find use for it," Giff's mother had said about the money. Of course, he would — if this weekend was the last time he was going to stay with them.

The thought worried him. How he'd like to stay! He had come to like the MacKenzies very much — more than he had ever liked anyone before. They were family. They had fun together. They joked, they laughed. Oh, sure, they argued some, and they disagreed some. But in the end they always resolved their differences. It was home, a kind of home in which there was friendship and love, things Peter had never really known, things he'd like to be part of very much.

So now, if he left, the reason would be different from the one that made him leave the Bentleys. He had run away from there purposely. He'd had to. But he didn't want to leave the MacKenzies. If he did, it would be because they asked him to go.

Peter thought he could easily see their side of it if they decided not to keep him. They already had two grown children. The cost of raising them was astronomical. After D.C. graduated from high school, she was going to attend a school to become an airline stewardess, and Giff might go to college, even though he'd said he wasn't sure what he wanted to do yet. But he was intelligent, and aggressive. He'd want to go. Probably to one of the more prestigious colleges in the country. That would mean a lot of money. Why would the MacKenzies want another kid in the family? Mr. MacKenzie's salary certainly wasn't so deep into the thousands that he and Mrs.

MacKenzie could support a third kid, even if Giff *didn't* go to college.

Peter found himself intimidated by these thoughts, and when he finally fell asleep he dreamed of being chased by someone whose face was hidden in shadow. The person was laughing a loud, crazy laugh and drawing closer to him. Peter tried to scream . . . to run faster . . . but the scream choked in his throat and his legs refused to move.

"Pete! Wake up!"

Someone was shaking him, and he woke, trembling and sweating. He looked up and saw Giff staring down at him, his blond hair disheveled.

"You must've had quite a nightmare, Pete," Giff said. "You all right now?"

"Yeah. I'm okay."

"Want a drink or something?"

"No. I'll be all right."

"Okay. See you at breakfast."

Giff tucked the covers under Peter's chin and around him, as if Peter were a kid brother, and he slept better the rest of the night.

The next morning at the breakfast table Peter told the family about his dream, confessing that he'd had that same dream — or a similar one — for as long as he could remember.

"I'm not surprised, Peter," Mr. MacKenzie said sympathetically. "You haven't had a very happy life, and your future is in question. It's no wonder. And nightmares can be scary. I have them now and then myself."

"Right," D.C. said, her eyes flashing with mischief. "When stocks take a big fall."

Everyone laughed at the way D.C. had turned the seriousness of the conversation into a joke — even if it wasn't a funny, rib-tickling one — and Peter wondered if he would ever learn enough about stocks to understand what was meant by "stocks taking a big fall," or, as he had heard Mr. MacKenzie say the other day, "a two-point jump in the Dow Jones average."

There were twenty-four entries that afternoon at the Bumble Bee Speedway, more than in any other moto in which Peter had competed. The number of bikes scared him. Twenty-four bikes meant that his chances of winning were pretty slim.

He was ninth from the end, Giff was sixth, and

D.C. fifth. Giff was wearing his usual blue gear and blue helmet, the number 11 prominent on the front number plate on the bike and on his helmet. And D.C. was in her crimson uniform, which she had washed the day before, giving it a brand-new look.

Peter felt like an old warrior in the scuffed orange uniform that Giff had worn during his early motocrossing days. But if he hadn't kept it, I might not be racing, Peter thought. Uniforms, or protective pants and jackets, helmets, face shields, and boots were a must in motocross competition.

Four other girls besides D.C. were racing, though Peter would not have known it if he had not heard their names announced over the public address system. In their uniforms and helmets they didn't look any different from the boys.

Three other names that he couldn't help hearing were Dexter Pasini, Jess Kutter, and Bill Rocco. This might be my last moto, Peter thought. He determined to do the best he could, and try to make those bums eat his dust as they had done a few times to him.

Promptly at twelve noon, the first twenty-minute heat got under way.

The gate dropped, and all twenty-four bikes rolled over it and headed for the hill. Peter climbed it with hardly any problem, except near the apex of it when the bike next to him almost collided into his as it clawed its way up. But Peter, turning the handlebars slightly to the left, succeeded in avoiding a collision, and seconds later he was roaring down the grade amid a thundering roar of engines and exhausts.

He was happy that the first treacherous obstacle was over, and felt inclined to see whether Giff and D.C. had made the hill, too. But he didn't dare look until he was safely on the level stretch, heading toward the first jump-hill just beyond the curve ahead.

Then he looked and saw both of them blazing down the track, their hands stretched out, gripping their handlebars, their helmeted heads crouched low, cutting down air resistance.

An instant later a bike crept up beside Peter, blocking his view, and he quickly turned his attention back to the track in front of him — but not before he recognized the familiar yellow fenders of a Corella.

Dex Pasini was pushing past Peter, his white-helmeted head bent as far down toward his handlebars as he could get it. Peter tried to ignore him but found that it was hard to ignore someone who was riding so close to you. They were almost hub to hub as they sailed over the jump-hill, soaring through space at the same time, then landing at the same time, as if the maneuver were planned.

Move, baby, move! Peter urged the Muni, realizing that the moment might have come when he could match Dex's skill, pass him, and stay ahead to win the race. His hands were like steel grips on the handlebars as he kept control of the bike.

Then came a short, bumpy stretch that had the tails of both bikes bobbing like rabbits, and then another jump-hill, which they both took with equal speed and eaglelike grace.

It was at the high berm that Dex Pasini, coming down from it with the throttle of his bike wide open, breezed by Peter and got ahead of him by at least two lengths. Peter's hope faltered and began to drain from him as he accelerated his bike and tried to close the gap between him and Dex again. But just then another bike, from Peter's left side, skidded toward Peter, forcing him to cut his speed slightly, thus giving Dex an additional advantage.

Dex was a skilled rider, Peter would be the first to admit, but luck was still riding with him, too.

Peter got a glimpse of Mr. MacKenzie holding up a pit board with a message on it for Giff — "5 — 19," which meant that Giff was in fifth place behind the leader, and that there were nineteen minutes left to go in the heat.

Mr. MacKenzie had promised to be D.C.'s pit-board man in the second heat, and regretted that there weren't three heats so that he'd be able to give Peter equal time.

"That's okay," Peter had told him. "I'll just try to do the best I can."

There were eight minutes left to go in the heat before Peter was able to catch up to Dex Pasini again. Dex, Peter figured, must have had some trouble that had caused him to lose ground.

Peter passed Dex as they zipped past the second berm on the track, his hopes of beating Dex soaring again as he remained ahead of Dex going toward the wide, right-hand curve. Peter roared up the high berm on the left side of the track, blazed down it toward the next berm, which was on the right-hand side now, then zoomed around the next two sharp curves that finally led him down the stretch toward the last hairpin curve of the track.

As Peter started to negotiate the inside curve of the hairpin, he saw a yellow-fendered bike creeping up on his right side, front wheel twisting back and forth in a short arc to keep the machine under control. The rider was Dex. And before the hairpin curve was behind them, Dex was in the lead again. Peter's lips tightened in anguish as he saw his hopes of beating Dex go up in smoke once more.

But it was a Suzuki that crossed the finish line first. Dex came in second, and Giff third. Peter finished fourth.

14

Third place! Not bad! That'll keep your points up!"

Giff smiled as he shook Peter's extended hand. "Thanks, Pete. You didn't do bad yourself."

"Yeah. But I'm still eating Pasini's dust," Peter said, realizing the very few times that he had made Dex eat his. "One of these days."

"We've been saying that for the last two years, Peter," D.C. chimed in, taking off her helmet and shaking her head to let her hair fall freely around it. "But coming in third and fourth isn't bad at all. Look at me. Sixth."

Peter shrugged. "Which isn't so bad, either, when you figure there were eighteen other riders shooting for the same target."

D.C. looked at him, her coffee-brown eyes twinkling. "No, not so bad, considering that I was eating *your* dust," she exclaimed.

She laughed, and he laughed, too. "Maybe next time," he said.

Giff grinned, and looked at Peter. "You know, she just might do it?" he said, making it sound like a question.

Peter agreed. He could not argue with Giff about that.

Only once during the break did a thought other than of the motocross enter Peter's mind. This is the weekend I'm supposed to find out if I stay with the MacKenzies or if they want me to leave. When am I going to find that out?

The thought triggered an ache in his stomach, and he turned away from Giff and D.C. to prevent them from seeing the look of despair that came into his eyes. Good thing there's a motocross, he told himself, or I'd go crazy wondering what the outcome would be.

Eighteen riders competed in the second heat. Six of the original twenty-four could not race because of various problems their machines had sustained.

By two o'clock, when the second heat started, the sky became cloudy and the air muggier than it had been that morning. A huge flock of sea gulls was soaring lazily over a field next to the track, and Peter worried that a storm was brewing and might wash out the moto.

But the storm didn't materialize, and the heat got under way.

He was in the fifth position from the right side of the starting line, sure as can be that the bike was in as good a shape as it was in the first heat. He had checked the carb, replaced the plug, filled the gas tank, and seen that the suspension forks were in excellent condition. Nervous and tense, he waited for the starting gate to drop.

The announcement came for the riders to start their engines. Peter turned the key in the ignition. The engine popped. Seventeen other bikes popped to life, too.

Then the gate dropped, and eighteen front wheels sprinted over the round pipe as the rear knobbies grabbed the dirt, churned, and propelled vehicles and riders forward. Peter found a line and remained on it as he shot the Muni up and over the hill, his heart singing as this first important feat was accomplished.

He leaned over as he headed down the stretch, his head and shoulders bent low, and pushed his weight back further on the seat to give the rear wheel all the traction it could get.

Rounding the first curve and making the first jump made him doubly grateful for the Boykins shock absorbers, which helped smooth out the bumps. The Muni 125 could really take it.

Peter negotiated the second jump with ease, then gunned the engine and headed for the first wide berm. About eight or nine bikes were in front of him, the first one leading by about two bike lengths. It was Dexter Pasini's Corella. Somehow Peter wasn't surprised.

Slightly ahead of him were D.C. and Giff, D.C. riding about a bike length ahead of her brother. What gumption, Peter thought. She could really ride, that was for sure.

As it was during the first heat, pit-board men stood at various corners of the track, each with an abbreviated message scrawled on his pit board. And this time, as he had promised, Mr. MacKenzie was giving his messages to D.C. on the board that he was holding up.

There was little change in the bikes' positions as the first lap ended, except that Dex had increased his lead from two bike lengths to three. Giff squeezed past D.C. on the third lap and got into fourth place behind Dex. D.C. held tenaciously on to sixth place, two lengths ahead of Peter, who found himself now being challenged by Bill Rocco, who had sneaked up on him at his left side.

Rocco crept up close to him as they headed for the high berm, and almost bumped into him as they came roaring down the incline.

He's trying to scare me, Peter thought. But I won't scare. Not this time. Not when this might turn out to be my last moto here in Cypress Corners.

He gunned the engine as they headed down the stretch toward the next berm and saw Rocco's Fitz RK wobble for a few seconds as if, for just a second or so, Rocco had lost control of it. The seconds were enough for Peter to surge ahead of him, and to overtake number 3 just before it reached the next left-turn berm.

Two laps later he saw a blue-tanked Yamaha sweep past him on the same high berm on which he had nearly collided with Rocco, and seconds later found himself eating D.C.'s dust.

He caught up to her as the moto went into its ninth minute — eleven minutes to go — and saw Giff about two lengths ahead of them. Only two riders were ahead of Giff: number 16, the Honda ridden by Rick Mendoza, a strong contender, and number 44, the Corella ridden by Dex Pasini.

With eight minutes left to go, Mendoza was hit with a problem. His rear tire blew as his machine took the track's first jump-hill and landed on it. The machine swerved dangerously across the track and smashed into the fence on the right-hand side. Mendoza escaped without a scratch.

With him out of the race, Dex took over the lead. Three lengths behind him was D.C.; two lengths behind her was Giff; and a half a length behind Giff was Peter.

"Come on, babe! Come on!" Peter whispered to the Muni. "You can do better than this! I know you can!"

With four minutes to go he swept ahead of Giff and began to creep up to D.C., who was now giving Dex the challenge of his career. Dex was only half a length ahead of her!

They were approaching the second berm when Peter, to the left and about a length behind D.C., cut to the outside of her. At the same time, Dex was *also* cutting to the right, and got in front of Peter.

"Darn you!" Peter thought, and accelerated the Muni. Hunched back on the seat to help give the rear tire all the traction possible, he aimed for the spot on Dex's right side. Hope ignited in him as he swept down the berm alongside of Dex.

Then Peter saw Dex squeezing up beside him, trying to force him to the inside. Just ahead was a left-hand turn that curved to the right farther on.

Peter knew that Dex was trying to scare him into slowing down and backing off, but he held his position and kept up his speed. Now that he was the closest he had ever been to beating Dexter, he was not going to give up that chance. No matter what Dex tried to do.

They headed side by side to the next berm, Peter

still on Dex's left side, and then shot down the short stretch toward the next smaller berm, one that headed into a brief hairpin curve.

They were still hub to hub as they shot into the hairpin, and then into the next short curve to the right — when the Corella rammed into the Muni.

Peter fought to control his balance and the bike as it headed for the fence on his left side. He ricocheted against it, got back on the track, and accidently rammed into the Corella. The Corella, still traveling at high speed, then crashed into the right-hand-side fence, behind which spectators suddenly screamed, yelled, and scrambled back to avoid being struck.

Peter, his feet dangling along the sides of the Muni to help maintain his balance, started to accelerate the machine again to keep his lead. It was now or never, he thought. What had happened was Dex Pasini's fault. Maybe that brief contact was an accident. But maybe it wasn't. Maybe Dex had wanted to make it *look* like an accident.

Whatever it was, I'm in the lead now, Peter thought, and I'm going to keep it.

Then he glanced back and saw Dex lying down on the track, trying to get up and apparently unable to. At that moment D.C. came sweeping around the curve, and two bike lengths behind her came Giff.

Dex is hurt, thought Peter. He could get hit. Maybe smashed up badly. Maybe killed.

Quickly he slowed down, stopped the bike, shoved it against the fence, and ran back to help Dex.

He saw D.C. and Giff both glance at Dex, then at him, and he thought for a second or two that they were slowing down.

"No!" he shouted, motioning them on. "Keep going! Keep going!"

They kept going, accelerating their bikes again as they headed down the track, and Peter rushed to Dex. Getting behind him and lifting him by the armpits, Peter pulled Dex to the fence and then under it as one of the spectators raised it up. Once they were safely out of the way of oncoming bikes, he paused and looked into the eyes that he could barely see through the dark visor of Dex's helmet.

He didn't know what to say. He heard shouts of "Finish the race, kid! Finish the race!" But he wanted to make sure that Dex was all right.

Dex's mouth opened. "You're crazy, Lewinski," he murmured. "You know that? You're really crazy. Why didn't you leave me there? You could've won the race hands down."

Peter looked at him squarely. "I'm satisfied just to have beaten you, Dex," he said calmly.

Then he got up, crawled back under the fence, ran to his bike, and went on to finish the race.

He came in thirteenth.

D.C. was first, Giff second, a Honda third, and a Suzuki fourth.

"I feel funny about the win," D.C. said as she, Giff, Peter, and her father headed home in the borrowed Ford pickup.

"Why?" said Mr. MacKenzie. "You won it fair and square. Why should you feel funny?"

She shrugged. "Peter should've won it."

"Don't feel bad," Peter said, smiling. "I'm happy enough to have been ahead of Dex when the accident happened. That was even more important to me than winning."

D.C. looked at him and frowned. "Peter Lewinski, you're crazy, you know that?"

He met her eyes squarely. "That's funny," he said. "Dex said the same thing."

Mrs. MacKenzie met them at the door. The moment Peter saw her happy face and met her warm, sparkling eyes, he knew that she had some important news.

"Guess what?" she said as she closed the door behind them.

"Oh, come on, Mother," D.C. exclaimed, unzipping her uniform. "We haven't time for guesses. Give us the news. Please?"

Peter waited, tense. All eyes were upon her.

"The Bentleys were here, Peter. They brought your suitcase with all your clothes in it."

His heart almost stopped. He tried to say something.

But he couldn't. He was afraid he'd cry if he tried.

Mrs. MacKenzie came forward, clutched his hands in hers. Tears glistened in her eyes.

"We had decided we wanted to keep you with us as far back as a week ago, Peter," she said tremulously. "But we weren't sure what the Bentleys might want to do. Then they came over this afternoon — Dr. and Mrs. Bentley. Not the boy. He preferred not to come. Anyway, we didn't talk very long. They had made their decision not to make a fuss about your staying here several days ago. They said they understand your feelings, and why you had run away. They're sorry, but they think as long as we can give you a good home, and companionship — something that they were not able to give you — they'll be pleased and happy. All we have to do now is to sign some papers to make it legal. Isn't that good news?"

"It's terrific!" he cried, and flung his arms around her. Then each of the others hugged him, and from D.C. he got a kiss.

"Now we have *three* racing champs in the family," D.C. exclaimed cheerfully. "How about that?"

"And a first-class mechanic," Giff added. "Don't forget that."

Peter laughed. He had never felt so good in his life. "Right," he said.

Matt Christopher®

Lance Armstrong	*Michael Jordan*
Kobe Bryant	*Mario Lemieux*
Terrell Davis	*Tara Lipinski*
Julie Foudy	*Mark McGwire*
Jeff Gordon	*Greg Maddux*
Wayne Gretzky	*Hakeem Olajuwon*
Ken Griffey Jr.	*Alex Rodriguez*
Mia Hamm	*Briana Scurry*
Tony Hawk	*Sammy Sosa*
Grant Hill	*Venus and Serena Williams*
Derek Jeter	*Tiger Woods*
Randy Johnson	*Steve Young*

The #1 Sports Series for Kids

MATT CHRISTOPHER®

Read them all!

*Previously published as *Crackerjack Halfback*